Golden Eye
and the
KILLER CAT

GOLDEN EYE
and the KILLER CAT

Judith Anne Moody

Illustrated by
Rita Schoenberger

Edited by
Maryvonne Farrand

Order this book online at www.trafford.com
or email orders@trafford.com

Most Trafford titles are also available at major online book retailers.

Printed in Victoria, BC, Canada.

ISBN: 978-1-4251-7684-6 (soft)
ISBN: 978-1-4251-7685-3 (ebook)

Our mission is to efficiently provide the world's finest, most comprehensive book publishing service, enabling every author to experience success. To find out how to publish your book, your way, and have it available worldwide, visit us online at www.trafford.com

Trafford rev. 11/6/2009

www.trafford.com

North America & international
toll-free: 1 888 232 4444 (USA & Canada)
phone: 250 383 6864 ♦ fax: 812 355 4082

Dedication
This book is dedicated to childhood and freedom and the true spirit of the First Nations people.

Acknowledgements
The author is pleased to acknowledge the assistance and support of the following people:
Gabe Haythornethwaite of the Qu'wutsun (Cowichan) Headquarters,
Dr. Michelle Corfield of the Nuu-chah-nulth (Nootka) Tribal Council,
Andrea Sanborn of U'mista - Kwakwaka'wakw (Kawkiutl) Cultural Centre,
Rita Schoenberger, Maryvonne Farrand, Anonda Berg,
The Red Deer, UBC, Vancouver and Fraser Valley Regional Libraries,
The Royal B.C. Museum,
Dora Swustus of the Qu'wutsun Cultural Centre,
and my family and friends in B.C. and Alberta.

Disclaimer
This book is primarily a work of fiction. Although the cultural information and legends have been carefully researched, the author claims no copyright to any First Nations legends. Names have been simplified for ease of young readers.

List of Chapters

List of Illustrations

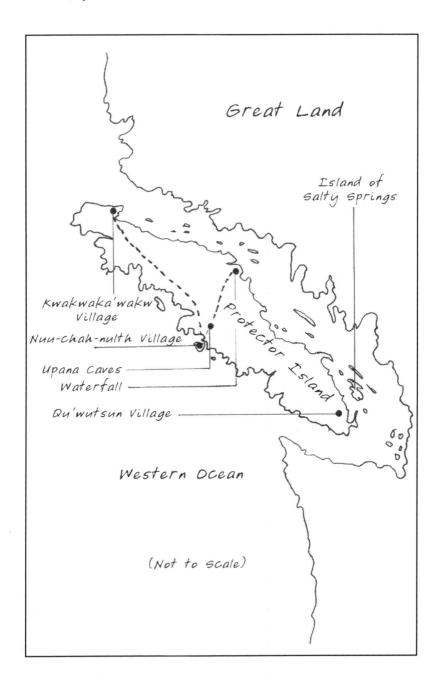

Chapter One

Paddling Song

Dip paddle, swing paddle, I am on my way,
Off to find adventure on this brand new day.
Sun on my paddle flashes oh so bright,
While I am paddling with all my might.
Hear me spirits of ancestors old,
You will be with me, so I am told.
Spirits of ocean, trees and the sky,
Strengthen my back as I am passing by.
Spirits of animals, fish and birds,
Whisper to me the empowering words.
Away I go now to places new,
Away with my friend in my small canoe.
Ocean uplift me, sky give me breath,
Sun give me warmth, earth give me rest.
I am Golden Eye, the Wolf-protected one,
I live for adventure, 'til the day is done.
Off to the land of my forbears I go,

Then on to others to learn more I know.
Big lands and new ways, new stories told,
Danger and adventure wait if I am bold.
Dip paddle, swing paddle, all through this day,
Golden Eye the mighty is on his way!

The time was many thousand years ago. The singer was Golden Eye, a Coast Salish boy of twelve summers. He sat straight-backed in his small canoe, his black hair brushing his strong, bronze-skinned shoulders. His face was fine-featured. His bright eyes, one brown, one wolf-gold, beneath the back-sloped forehead of the high-born, took in everything: water depth, wind strength, passing birds and the strength of the sun – all things that would determine how this day's traveling would go.

His sturdy companion Tan Buck yelled forward, "That's a great paddling song. Did you just make that up?" Tan Buck's powerful muscles rippled and his happy face beamed as he drove his paddle into the chilly green ocean, powering the canoe ahead.

"Yes," Golden Eye called back over his shoulder. "It just came to me, like Uncle Raven Claw said while he was making me this excellent canoe. He said 'Listen to the spirits when you travel away and they will help you make your very own paddling song.'"

"Well, he was right. Which bay are we heading

for anyway? There are so many on Protector Island."

"Let's stop paddling for a minute and look around. Look back! There's our home, the Island of Salty Springs, on the right. Off to the north of it, there's Long Nose Island and behind it Oyster Shell Island and all the smaller ones in between. Can't even see Long Bone Island because Crouching Mountain's in the way. And way across the wide stretch of water, on the Great Land, you can just see our favourite mountain – the one that looks like…"

"Like it's wrapped in one of our mothers' goat fur blankets. Yes! That old, smoking volcano! And look. You can hardly see the Thousand-Mountains-in-a-Row for all those low clouds around their bottoms!"

"And ahead of us on the left is the Saanich peninsula where there are many Salish villages. Hey, look! There's smoke from the morning fires of the Tsawout. I really like their village with the foreshore full of reeds and grasses, that wide sandy beach and those strange piles of rocks. We've played many games there, haven't we?

We have to turn right now, not turn into any of those big bays. We're to head up this inner coast of Protector Island until we see our cousin Big Head waiting on the beach. See how the coast rears up to high cliffs now? Get ready, we're going to pass through Sansum Narrows now."

"Thank goodness we're at slack tide. Remember

the morning you were leaving for your vision quest, how strong the tide ran through there, and that huge whirlpool that nearly sucked us in?"

"I remember all right," said Golden Eye, with his jaw set grimly.

Just then, a big, spraying fountain of seawater geysered up beside the canoe as up from the depths rose Black Fin, Golden Eye's young killer whale friend! His sleek, wet, black and white body glistened in the sun and his tall, black dorsal fin cut through the air as he leapt in an arc and dove back under the ocean.

"Hello boy! What are you doing here?" yelled Tan Buck.

"I'll bet he wants to come along on our adventure," said Golden Eye, grinning with happiness to see his orca friend again. "It's good to have you with us, little Wolf-of-the-Sea. Welcome!"

Black Fin leapt straight up, twenty feet in the air, and came down on his side causing a huge splash that drenched the boys and left a considerable amount of salty water in the bottom of the canoe.

Tan Buck wiped his face and while he bailed out the canoe with their maple-wood bailer, Golden Eye dove into the water and swam with his orca friend – sometimes beside him, sometimes on top of him – holding fast to Black Fin's dorsal fin – diving and splashing and enjoying the sparkling green coldness of the sea.

Golden Eye's mind flashed back to the day he met Black Fin – the first time they swam together. Never had Golden Eye experienced such complete joy, followed by such fear and danger as on that day this past summer when he was attacked by the uncle who tried to kill him! He had survived thanks to his two friends, Tan Buck and Black Fin and by using his spirit powers. Golden Eye shook off such thoughts and enjoyed his swim with Black Fin for a few more minutes; then hauled himself back into his canoe.

"We're off on another adventure, Black Fin," he called to the young killer whale. "Don't get too far from your pod now. I'll bet your mother worries just like mine does."

So on through the Sansum Narrows the boys paddled, past the ancient watery lair of Shu-Shu-Cum, The Hungry One. According to an old legend Shu-Shu-Cum had swallowed many Coast Salish people before having his snout crushed by a massive rock tossed from the Great Land by Sum-Ul-Quatz, the giant.

Black Fin breached once more then turned around and swam back to his pod, playfully accompanied by a pair of frisky porpoises.

Golden Eye's mind wandered back again as he paddled in perfect rhythm with Tan Buck. He thought back to the summer when the two friends had experienced so much. The western shore of their home, the Island of Salty Springs, slipped past on their right. It was the land where they had grown from infancy to strong young men. Memories of games and adventures rushed through his mind as the ocean rushed beneath his canoe. He could feel the spirits of his father and mother, Grey Fox and Whispering Dawn, enfolding him with love, those of his shaman-grandfather Strong Oak, his medicine woman grandmother Robin Song, and all the ten families of their village wishing him well on his journey.

Some memories were exciting, like finding the cave that held not only gold nuggets but also an evil spirit that had to be vanquished. Memories like getting this, his first canoe, climbing Crouching Mountain with Tan Buck and seeing the world around them. Days of running with Tan Buck and with his friend and protector Old One Eye, the wolf came to his mind.

He remembered the sounds, excitement and tragedy of the Great Potlatch and then the fun of the children's own potlatch. Some memories were more dreadful: the death of Ten Trees, the attempts on his own life - right up to the day of his vision quest. His protecting wolf spirit had warned him and saved him on that day.

Old One Eye. A tear welled in Golden Eye's eye and he took a moment to rest his hand on the pelt and head of his old friend who had not wakened one morning, his spirit having departed. Golden Eye's father had very carefully skinned the old wolf, keeping the emptied head attached, and his mother had carefully tanned it. Now it served as both blanket and talisman for their son.

With a deep breath Golden Eye shook off his sadness and began to look forward to making new friends and new memories. After a summer of helping with the village's food gathering and storage, they were on their way. First they planned a visit with relatives in the Qu'wutsun village, their ancestral home on Protector Island, then on up to where they would part.

Halfway up Protector Island, Tan Buck would meet with an envoy from the great Kwakwaka'wakw people of the northeast corner of Protector Island and carry on to their village. He had pledged to carry back to that village the bones of a Kwakwaka'wakw visitor who had perished in a fall. Golden Eye, however, was on a mission to traverse Protector Island and meet with the Nootka people, the whale hunters of the mid-west coast of Protector Island. After that he would cross the island diagonally and meet up with Tan Buck before heading home.

At Potlatch his cousin Big Head from Protector Island had told Golden Eye tales of traveling with other Salish people on the trails across Protector Island to trade with the people of the west coast. Golden Eye had been fascinated, hearing of the bravery of the Nootka people, who set out into the vast, stormy, endless Western Ocean to actually hunt the giant whales that passed by each spring and autumn. The Salish people hunted seals and sea lions but never anything so vast as ocean-going whales, although if one washed ashore they certainly took advantage of this great good luck.

Golden Eye could hardly wait to see this phenomenon. It was the ninth moon so whale migration could be expected soon. But first they must paddle on, past the great cliff, to where the shore flattened out onto a gravel beach and there they would meet up with Big Head.

Chapter Two

Big Head and the First Men Legends

"Over here. Here's a nice sandy spot," yelled Big Head.

Tan Buck and Golden Eye deftly turned the canoe and paddled up to the beach. They were careful not to dig too deep with their paddles so that they didn't shatter them on the rocks at the bottom.

Big Head grabbed the prow of the canoe and pulled it near the shore. The boys jumped out onto the sand. Big Head, older than them by several summers, lifted one side of the canoe and Golden Eye and Tan Buck lifted the other. Then they rushed up and set the canoe down, well above the high tide line.

"It's good to see you boys. What took you so long? I've been waiting here for an hour," cried the big fellow.

"Ahh, Golden Eye had to go for a swim with his pet killer whale again," explained Tan Buck.

"You have a pet killer whale?" cried Big Head in amazement.

"I'm lucky to be on good terms with most animals," said Golden Eye, "especially wolves. That's my protector spirit and orcas are the wolves of the sea so I guess it's just natural."

"Natural for you maybe, but, come to think of it, you'll fit right in with the Nootka, wait and see," said Big Head mysteriously. "Come on now. The families of my village are waiting to see you and hear the news of your families. There'll be a big feast tonight and I can hardly wait. I'm still a growing boy you know and I'm always hungry."

Golden Eye and Tan Buck gazed at their cousin who stood head and shoulders taller than them and had a head truly larger than any they had ever seen! They were not surprised that he was always hungry. They were feeling a little famished themselves, not having eaten since their early breakfast of berries and fresh spring water.

Big Head turned to lead the way, bumped his head on a low branch, ducked, caught his foot on an exposed root and fell headfirst into a mud puddle. He rolled onto his backside and looked up at Golden Eye and Tan Buck - mud and water dripping off his face onto his chest. He began to shout with laughter. They couldn't help it – try as they might to keep it in, Golden Eye and Tan Buck exploded in laughter at the sight.

Big Head blinked, shook his head and wiped the mud from his eyes and nose and spit mud from his mouth. Pretty soon all three of them were rolling on the ground, helpless with laughter. When they finally ran out of breath and stopped laughing, Big Head crawled over to a stream and washed himself off. Then they all leapt into the ocean for a refreshing swim and had another rinse in the stream, after which they all stood dripping wet on the shore.

"We're sorry for laughing at you, Big Head, but you looked so funny – like your face was melting off," said Golden Eye, trying not to start laughing again.

"Yes," Tan Buck joined in, "I'm sorry too." He did, however, have to clap his hand over his mouth to keep from breaking out laughing again.

"That's okay cousins," said Big Head. "I've been living with the drawbacks of my extra size all my life. It would be all right if I wasn't clumsy too. My big feet always seem to find anything there is to trip over, and I practically have to crawl into the doors of our longhouses. I had a more or less permanent bruise on my forehead – like this one coming up – until I adjusted to my size."

All three boys had another good long chuckle about this and then collapsed onto the grass to catch their breath. They watched as beautiful white clouds sailed overhead – some shaped like big canoes piled high with fluffy cargo, some like arrows or running ferrets, some resembling huge bowls of snowy berries.

"Is Big Head your real name?" asked Tan Buck boldly as Golden Eye gave him a sharp look meaning 'don't be so nosy'.

"Oh no. Like everyone else I started out with one name when I was a baby, got changed to another one when I was six summers old and another one at my vision quest potlatch. I'll decide on my grownup name when or if something really big happens to me, or I'll choose one from an ancestor. But generally everyone calls me Big Head because of my size and this big noggin of mine. Well, come on, let's get going to the village."

"I could use a good run – to stretch my legs and to dry off too," said Golden Eye.

With that, the three boys set off, Big Head in the lead. Beyond the first row of shrubs near the shore a great valley opened before them. Although the two travelers were used to the sight of the beautiful valley to the west of Crouching Mountain on the Island of Salty Springs, they couldn't help but draw a sharp breath at what they saw. Spreading westward was a massive lush valley, gently rolling from the far-off mountains down to the sea and split by a tumbling, splashing river. This river itself was fed by numerous streams and rivulets gurgling down from the two local mountains. Off in the distance sparkled crystal blue lakes ringed with poplar trees. Enormous oak and maple trees sheltered the land too, interlaced with stands of evergreens. The world already seemed much bigger to Golden Eye.

After a while the three boys stopped for a break and helped themselves to handfuls of huckleberries from a bush beside them.

"You see that mountain over there?" asked Big Head. "That's where the first Coast Salish man came down to earth. Saghalie Tyee, the Great Spirit, looked down through the clouds and saw this wonderful place, full of deer, elk, bears, and birds; and the salmon leaping up the river chased by whales, porpoises and seals. He thought this place needed some balance between the land and the sea so he sent down a man. He gave him a fine spirit and a good mind – made him smaller than the largest creature but bigger than the smallest and taught him many things.

He showed him how to make a weir to trap salmon, steelhead and trout on the rivers, how to trap deer with nets and bears in pits and how to make use of all their parts for food, blankets and clothing too. He taught him to use the mighty cedar to make his home, clothing and medicines. He taught him to walk lightly on the earth, taking only what he needed, using all of it, and being respectful and thankful for its bounty.

At night though, when he heard the call of the loon on the water, the first man, whom we call Syalutsa, became lonely, wondering if he would always be the only person on earth. He shouldn't have worried because pretty soon another young man showed up, named Stutsun. They became brothers and Syalutsa taught him all he knew and then sent him off on a spirit quest.

'You must bathe in every stream, lake and river that you come to – never miss even one,' Syalutsa instructed Stutsun. 'This will help make your spirit strong. Sleep every night under a cedar tree with your feet facing East. Keep your spirit open for lessons but never reveal these secrets to anyone. Do not show fear under any circumstances, no matter what you may experience. Now go. May the Great Spirit be with you. I hope I will see you again.'"

"Did he see him again?" asked Tan Buck, wide-eyed.

"Oh yes, he did return after several years with some great stories to tell."

"Like what?"

"Stories of strange beasts! Stutsun came to a lake and was bathing when a gigantic two-headed snake came lashing and splashing across the lake toward him. The water churned and boiled and the creature lunged toward him, first with one of its horrible heads then with the other, sunlight flashing off its great big scales. Stutsun remembered his brother saying, 'Have no fear, no matter what' so he stood still in the face of the creature until it finally backed off and disappeared into the lake. Then a great wind blew across the lake, blowing Stutsun's hair straight back and nearly knocking him off his feet.

'What did you feel? What did you do?' asked Syalutsa.

'I felt amazed but at peace. That creature and I both have our place on earth, so why should I kill it?' he asked his brother.

'Another time, I was sleeping under a cedar tree, early in the morning, when I felt something pass over me. I opened my eyes and saw two astounding birds.

One was a mystical Firebird of great size and wingspread, his many-coloured feathers flashing in the sun. Beside it flew a Singing Bird, not so big nor so bright but singing in a magical voice – almost human and so clear – whose song echoed through the forest all through that day. Again, I was not scared.

On another day I stepped into a small valley and was suddenly confronted by another two-headed beast, a flying one this time. He was absolutely huge, half filling the sky, and with flames shooting from his beak. I knew then that he was the younger brother of Thunderbird but again I stood still and straight, knowing no fear. And so that horrible bird flapped away, flattening the grasses with the wind from his wings.

Then just last week I was bathing in a lake to the north of here when a really big, blue-green creature began to churn up the lake as it came zig-zagging toward me, under the surface. I tried to draw it nearer by slowly backing toward the shore of the lake but it was not to be fooled. So, not wanting to show itself and not having drawn me into the depths of the lake, it, whatever it was, disappeared, leaving the lake all foamy and choppy with waves. Once again, a great wind arose and roared across the lake toward me, knocking me onto the shore.'

'Were you afraid of that blue-green monster?' asked Syalutsa

'No my brother. As you told me, I showed no fear and the fearful things went away.'

'Well, what lessons of the spirits did you learn on your journey?'

'Oh, no,' chuckled Stutsun, 'you won't catch me on that either. The last thing you said was never to tell ANYONE the things I learned, and that means YOU TOO!'"

"Wasn't Syalutsa lonely again when his brother went off?" Golden Eye wondered out loud.

"Oh, he was for a while but that's another story. Syalutsa began thinking he would like a wife; someone who would cook the food he brought home, someone to make his clothes, and someone to talk to. So, he carved himself a wooden wife and sat her by the fire. Every day he brought home fish and game and put them before her. Every day he talked to her, asking her how she was and telling her of his daily excursions and explorations, but she never cooked and she never talked.

However, the daughter of another of the first people sent down from above had heard from her father of this fine, handsome young man in this great valley so she traveled there with her maid. They kept hidden and watched Syalutsa. Then one day they crept up to his lodge and saw within it the wooden wife, silent by the fire, food and skins sitting useless before her. The chief's daughter knew that she would make a much better wife for Syalutsa and so she made a plan. That day she slipped inside the lodge and cooked up the food, then went and hid in the forest. Syalutsa was absolutely delighted to see that his wooden wife had at last done something useful. He had been getting fed up with her silence and lack of work.

The next day, waiting until Syalutsa was far away again, the young woman again slipped into his lodge and made for him some wonderful garments and blankets from the animal skins sitting before the wooden wife. Once more, Syalutsa was thrilled to come home and find that Wooden Wife had made herself useful. But yet she did not speak to him so he was still lonely for the sound of another human's voice.

Finally, on the next day, the young woman posted her maid as a lookout and went into the lodge. She cooked the food, flavouring it with herbs from the woods, she tanned the hides and then she threw the wooden wife into the fire! Then she sat down in the place of the wooden wife. When Syalutsa arrived, he exclaimed over the fine food and the tanned hides.

'Thank you very much, Wooden Wife,' he said.

'You're welcome,' said the young woman.

Well, Syalutsa was startled and amazed and overjoyed! He picked up the young woman and found that Wooden Wife had come to life. She was flesh and blood like him. Once again he was filled with joy, but just then he looked into the fire-pit and saw there the hand of Wooden Wife. He began to scream and cry and threatened to kill the young woman until she said to him, 'Isn't a real woman so much better than a wooden one? Who do you think has been cooking your food and making your garments and robes? Wooden Wife was good for nothing but firewood, don't you agree?'

Syalutsa stopped ranting and raving and thought

about it. Finally, he had to agree with her. Even though he had spent many evenings talking to Wooden Wife and wishing for her to become real, it became clear to him that that was never going to happen. He realized he should be thankful to the Great Spirit for sending him a real wife."

"I had heard that the first man came from our ancestral home here on Protector Island, but that's the first time I really heard the whole story," said Golden Eye in an awed voice. "You're a pretty good story teller, aren't you Big Head?"

"Thank you! I love to hear a good story and I love to tell them to someone new too. I love to watch their faces when they hear them - their eyes opening wide."

"Golden Eye tells a fine story too," Tan Buck said. "Maybe he'll tell one at your village."

"That would be great," replied Big Head. "After evening meal is the best time for stories, so let's get going."

The boys rose to carry on to the village but they all stopped dead in their tracks, the hair standing up on their necks, as they heard a great screaming snarl coming from the nearby evergreen forest.

"What on earth was that?" whispered Tan Buck, shivering in spite of himself.

"Let's run, boys," Big Head entreated. "That's the great big cougar that's been haunting this place for months now. He's got the personality of a deranged killer. He likes to pick off isolated targets and we might be considered fair game to him so let's get to the safety of the village as fast as we can!"

"What's a cougar like?" Tan Buck asked as he ran. "We've heard of them but never seen one."

"It's a mountain lion, a huge cat. If you know what a bobcat looks like, they're like that only many times their size and with no tufts on their ears. And teeth! The Great Spirit gave him enough teeth to take down an elk with one bite of its throat!"

"Are we close to the village yet?" Golden Eye asked, hopefully.

"Nearly there, cousins. See? You can see the tops of our longhouses over that ridge."

"Thank the Great Spirit," muttered Tan Buck, putting on another burst of speed.

Golden Eye and Tan Buck stretched their legs, trying to keep up with Big Head in the race to his village. Their minds were whirling as they tried to envision a mountain lion. How big was it? How long were its legs and how sharp were its claws? Did it kill humans – and for what? – sport or food? Most importantly, was it chasing them now?

A pair of pintail ducks whizzed past their heads, giving the boys more cause for alarm. Were they escaping from the beast too? A rabbit leapt up and away directly in Tan Buck's path, causing him to falter.

He jumped to the left, fell and rolled onto the ground. Big Head grabbed Tan Buck by his extended arm and swung him over his shoulder without even breaking stride! Golden Eye was hot on Big Head's heels and could hardly keep from bursting out laughing at the sight of Tan Buck's head bouncing off Big Head's back.

Finally, the Qu'wutsun village came into view as they passed over the crest of a grassy hill. Big Head slowed his pace to a jog and flipped Tan Buck onto his feet now that safety was near, preserving Tan Buck's dignity as he entered the village. Golden Eye took in the sight of the village – his ancestral home - on a shelf-like bank above the shores of the rushing river. His eyes followed the river to a mountain waterfall, visible off to the west. The village itself was a very large settlement that spread out in a vast arc on the bank. Five, no, eight, no, ten longhouses he counted! The largest had to be a hundred paces long and easily more than half that wide. Besides the longhouses there were quite a number of smaller buildings – sheds for salmon smoking and storing, for nets, and women's huts.

A crew of men was busy building yet another longhouse. The massive upright logs that would support the roof could still be seen as the long, incredibly straight-grained wall planks were slotted horizontally between upright posts, one above the other, and secured with cedar withes - strong strips of inner bark. The sound of chopping carried to them from another group of men. They were grooving the very long roof boards that would fit together, flange to flange, to keep them in place and to carry the rain away to the lower roof edges.

Big Head let out a mighty holler that drew everyone's attention. At once all the villagers stopped their tasks and came out – men, women and children – to greet the visitors. The great chief waited at the doorway to his longhouse, as his ceremony chief sprinkled eagle down on the path leading the boys up to him. The doorway itself resembled the gaping mouth of a giant black bear. The Great Chief stepped back into the longhouse and sat on his raised platform at the back of the house. Everyone else followed the three boys in and settled themselves along the platforms ringing the big house.

"Welcome to you, Golden Eye," announced the Ceremony Chief. "We have heard of your wonderful spirit powers – your blessings from the Great Spirit – and of your protection by the spirits of the wolves of the forest and of orca, the sea-wolf. We welcome you in honour of your chieftain father Grey Fox, your good mother Whispering Dawn, your grandfather, the shaman Strong Oak, and your grandmother, the wise medicine woman Robin Song. Stories of your power to turn back a forest fire, to become invisible to the great bear and to take shapes when in danger, have come to us from travelers. We are happy to welcome such a special one to our lodges and our fires.

Welcome also to your friend and companion Tan Buck, who we are told came to your rescue without thinking of his own safety. Welcome to you both. We are honored by your visit."

Golden Eye spoke then. "We are also greatly honored by such a wonderful welcome and bring greetings from all the families on the Island of Salty Springs. We have brought you gifts, including these big black mushrooms that grew after the big fire. See how they look like black brains? They really are delicious and the baskets they are in are the finest our women could weave. See the fine patterns? Please accept these gifts from your island cousins and thank you again for this warm welcome."

The Great Chief, Mountain Walker, then spoke. "Will you stay long with us, Golden Eye and Tan Buck?"

"Just a few days, I'm afraid," replied Golden Eye. "Tan Buck is on a mission to return the bones of a Kwakwaka'wakw man to his people. I have felt a call to visit the Nootka people out on what I hear is the wild west coast of Protector Island. We will travel up the east side by canoe until we meet a Kwakwaka'wakw boy, halfway up-island. There, Tan Buck will continue on with him while I go across-island to meet the great whalers of the Western Ocean."

"There are trading paths from here across the island, you know," offered Elk Hunter, the Ceremony Chief, "but if you wish to accompany your fine friend here halfway to the Kwakwaka'wakw nation, there is a waterway you can follow from there. A great salmon river runs far into Protector Island and the lake from which it flows will carry you even further on your journey. You will find small canoes at each end of the lake, left for travelers like yourself. Then there are rivers and streams to follow the rest of the way to the great inlet from the Western Ocean too, and a canoe to take you the rest of the way to the Nootka nation – the ocean whalers," offered another village elder.

"Be sure you stop at the Upana caves just before the inlet. They are really something to see," offered one of the house-builders, his adze resting across his knees. "There's an old hermit shaman living in one of them. It may even be his spirit that is calling you."

"There is a legend that Protector Island broke off from the Great Land far to the south, where it is warm all the time. The land has much limestone, the kind of stone that running and dripping water can shape into caves quite easily," offered a young hunter. "There are some caves up by the great salmon river too but nothing like those at Upana."

"Well, if the legend is true, I hope Protector Island is well anchored now and doesn't go floating off again someday," said Golden Eye. "It makes me dizzy just thinking about it."

Everyone in the longhouse had a good laugh at that.

"There is a beautiful waterfall somewhere near that river that you should see, just inland a short run. It is said to have a spirit living behind it. With your spirit power you might be able to contact it," offered an old grandmother of the village.

"One thing I'd like to know," asked Tan Buck, warmed by their hospitality, "did all the brothers who fell from the sky land here in what you call the warm land?"

"Oh no," answered Chief Mountain Walker, "some landed over on the Great Land. Some at the mouth of the mighty Sto'lo River, some far up the river in the interior of the Great Land, and some up the coast of the Great Land. We are a large nation – so large that our Halkomelem language sometimes sounds a little different coming from the mouths of the different groups. However, we all understand when it comes to trading and potlatching and arranging marriages, don't we?" he said, looking around at his people, who nodded in agreement.

"Yes," retorted Big Head. "Especially when it comes to food! And speaking of food, what's for dinner tonight. I'm starving after saving these two young pups from the Killer Cat."

Everyone was chuckling over Big Head's well-known huge appetite but they showed their concern about the cougar, asking if the boys had seen it or been attacked.

"No and no," answered Golden Eye. "But its scream or growl or whatever you call it made all my hair stand straight up. What do they look like, anyway?" he asked.

The village shaman, whose name was Lion Slayer, reached up to a shelf in his family's section of the longhouse and pulled down a rolled-up fur. He rolled it out before the boys and they both took a sharp intake of breath as it was revealed. Short, reddish, golden-tan fur stretched nearly a full man's length from the head that reminded the boys of a lynx or bobcat, but bigger – much bigger – and without ear tufts or stripes or spots except for black patches on the side of its nose. A mouth full of large teeth meant for tearing flesh gave them as much fear as the big, clawed paws. A furry tail, nearly as long as the beast itself, stretched out behind it.

The two travelers felt another thrill of fear as they imagined the massive muscles that had powered those big legs and the long back of the enormous cat. Then a toddling baby came over and rolled himself in the fur.

"Soft," he crooned.

And so the spell of fear was broken.

Chapter Three

Battle of the Monsters

"Come on. Let's go outside and play some games 'til evening meal is ready," called Big Head. "I saw a shooting star last night and that means that I and my team will win!"

"You think so, do you?" asked Eagle Feather, a boy of fourteen summers who was Big Head's usual rival at games. "I saw lightning before dawn this morning, and that means I and my team will win!"

"We'll see about that," laughed Big Head as he bumped his head on the opening of the longhouse and made a complete backward roll before coming to rest on his backside, shaking his head. Gales of laughter rippled through the crowd of Coast Salish children. Two big boys grabbed Big Head's arms and hoisted him upright.

"Girls over here," called an older girl, "six to a circle we'll play Ball in Air. Here, each of you, here's a ball on a thong. You have to hold the end of the thong with one hand only, waist high, and kick the ball up. Either foot, it doesn't matter, but never let it touch the ground and you can't go outside this circle I'm drawing. If you step out, you're out, or if your ball touches the ground, you're out. Winners from each circle will play off against each other to see who's the grand champion."

"Women over here," called Rabbit Skinner, a lean but well-muscled, athletic looking young woman. "We'll play Captive Ball. Same kind of ball on a two-steps-long thong, but you have to keep it in the air by hitting it with your other hand – no using the thong-holding hand. Miss once and you're out and you get to make dinner!"

"Boys over here," yelled Eagle Feather. "We'll play Turn Stick. How many of us are there? Four, eight, twelve. All right, three teams of four each, two facing two, ten paces apart. Here, each of you take one of these good, straight, three-steps-long sticks with one end dyed. First round, stand the plain end on one palm and flip it up so it makes a half turn and you catch it on the painted end. Second round, flip it to make a double flip and catch the plain end again. Third round, the stick must make one and a half flips so you catch the painted end.

Fourth round, two complete flips but before you throw you must say 'Two turns make I' or you're out.

Every round after that you have to say out loud how many flips you're going to make and then you have to make that many or you're out. Anyone dropping his stick or hitting anyone else's stick, or not making the right number of flips is out immediately. Last one standing from each team will play off 'til we know who's the best flipper today. We'll have one uncle watch each team just to make sure you do it right. Ready? Begin!"

The sweet afternoon air was soon filled with laughter, yells and groans as the competitors struggled to stay in the games. Yet even when they were eliminated the people cheered on their family members and friends, down to the battles of the champions. When the final grand champions were named, each after mighty performances and very stiff competition, the whole village gave out loud cheers. They thumped the winners on their backs amid calls of "I'll beat you next time!" and "You think so? You know I'm the best – better just admit it!"

Golden Eye and Tan Buck had done their best but had been eliminated late in the games, although Golden Eye had amazed the boys by causing his stick to hang suspended in the air for a moment while he brushed some flying dust from his left eye. They congratulated the winners heartily.

As the sun began to settle behind the mountains to the West, spreading a warm glow over the village, the breeze stopped as it did at this time most days, and even the birds became quieter as a sense of evening-time coming on filled the atmosphere.

"What's for dinner?" called the always hungry Big Head, causing everyone to chuckle. "I'm serious. We have special guests and we need to feed them properly."

"Here it comes," called out Many Blankets, the chief's wife. This name was given to her because it had taken many, many blankets to convince her father to let her go to marry Mountain Walker. She and the other women proceeded to carry out miniature canoes filled to their brims with fine food. Codfish, seal meat, steamed seaweed, smoked oysters, clams and baked roots of camas and bulrush were served in abundance and washed down with lots of clear spring water or salal tea. Fresh huckleberries were passed around in bowls carved with designs of various birds, fish and mammals. Everyone took a seat on one of the great logs around the central outdoor campfire place and dug into the food with gusto, all memory of games competition forgotten.

"No salmon, that's weird," Tan Buck leaned over and whispered in Golden Eye's ear.

"You're right," Golden Eye whispered back. "There should be lots of fresh chum salmon now. I wonder why they haven't caught any in all those weirs in the river."

Their whispers floated into the ear of Finder-of-the-Great-Spring, Big Head's uncle.

"You've learned of our shame and sorrow," he said.

The rest of the village grew silent and everyone stopped eating. Heads drooped and some of the men squirmed anxiously on their log seats.

"We have not been able to take any salmon for several days now," the older man intoned sadly.

"Why not?" piped up Tan Buck as Golden Eye elbowed him, trying to shush him. The people of the village all looked so woebegone that Golden Eye felt sorry for them before even hearing what was wrong. One young child started crying softly – seeing all the sad faces.

"Forgive my friend, his tongue wags with no restraint," uttered Golden Eye as Tan Buck gave him a little shove.

"There is nothing to forgive," replied Finder-of-the-Great-Spring. "For many days now Qwunus, a monstrous supernatural killer whale, has been blocking the mouth of our river, gobbling up all the salmon that usually come upstream to our weirs. Now, we don't expect our orca brothers to go without salmon to fill their bellies, but this one seems to want them all for himself. Even when he is full he remains at the mouth of the river, keeping the salmon out."

"We have prayed and chanted, night and day, to

the Great Spirit, Saghalie Tyee, for help and to the spirit of the orca himself to beg him to allow the salmon to come up the river," explained Mountain Walker.

"What will we eat in the winter if we have no salmon to smoke?" cried out Weaver Woman. "That whale must leave soon or we may all die before the moons of winter are past!"

Many voices rose in concern, explaining, complaining, arguing about the best way to deal with the situation.

"Quiet, everyone!" cried out an ancient, white-haired elder; a man wrapped in a thick brown blanket, which he clutched with his left hand, hiding his withered right arm. "I, Lion Slayer, shaman of this village, have determined a way to rid us of this angry whale. We have with us as our guest one who is strong with the spirits. One who can turn back forest fires and who can help rescue lost souls from the spirit world. Golden Eye, son of Grey Fox, will you lend your spirit powers to our prayers?

It came to me in a dream that we should pray to the Great Thunderbird who nests on that, the highest mountain on Protector Island and beg him to use his great power to defeat that greedy whale. Golden Eye, young though you are, we know you are strong with the spirits. Will you help us with our prayers?"

Golden Eye looked into Tan Buck's eyes,

wondering silently if they could really mean this. What a lot of responsibility this was, to help save the lives of a whole big village, to call down the mighty Thunderbird to fight a giant killer whale. Did they realize that he was only a boy of twelve summers, a boy from a small village on the Island of Salty Springs? Now, away from home and all that was familiar, Golden Eye felt small and young and inadequate. But how could he say no? These people were in such distress and they had welcomed him and his friend so warmly. Tan Buck stared back at Golden Eye and then spoke.

"You brought me back from the spirit world, my friend. You saved your brother from the jaws of Old Crooked Paw, the bear, and you changed into a seal to escape from the harpoons and arrows of Screaming Jay and even killed him at your spirit quest. Go on, you can do this! At least you can try - you know - add your power to theirs and see if you all can do it together."

That was all the encouragement he needed. Golden Eye stood up, his wolf skin around his shoulders, and said loudly, "I, Golden Eye, protected by the wolf spirits, and blessed by the Great Spirit, will be proud to pray and chant with you. I am getting a feeling, a vision inside my head, of a great battle ahead. I smell blood and I feel feathers floating down. This is a sign I think, that we will succeed. Let us join our spirits in this important quest."

The elders, the chiefs of each longhouse and the Great Chief, the medicine men and women and the shamans, young and old, rose and began to gather together. They all headed toward the big sweat lodge at the western edge of the village, overlooking the rushing, splashing river.

So, as Golden Eye followed the chiefs and shamans into the sweat lodge, the rest of the people of the village prepared for the night. The children chased each other and the dogs around the longhouses in one last burst of energy. Tan Buck and the other older boys went for a stroll up the river and the women and older girls cleaned up after the meal while the oldest men and women sat chatting around the lowering fire.

Golden Eye knew from his experiences back home that sweat lodge time could be a time of healing, of purification, of preparation for a big hunt, a voyage, or a rite of passage such as his vision quest. This time, however, he could sense the urgency, the deep importance, almost fear, among these people. As the elders seated themselves in a circle around the fire, Golden Eye took a moment to look into the faces of his companions.

"These are good people," he thought, "wise men and women who carry the burden of the safety and well-being of all the people of this great village, but they are worried, as would my own elders be, if the salmon – that wonderful gift of the Great Spirit-stopped coming to our rivers."

Water was splashed onto the hot rocks around the fire and huge billows of steam arose and filled the sweat lodge, which was a small version of a longhouse but with a low ceiling, close walls and a big animal hide hung in the doorway to keep the steam inside. The elders shucked off their capes, woven of softened inner cedar bark, and began to breathe in the cedar-scented steam. A very old man, his face a spiderweb of wrinkles, began a chant:

"Come Spirit of the Thunderbird, who nests in the dead volcano. Come Thunderbird, maker of thunder and lightning. Hear the voices of the People of the Salmon. Hear our prayers. Hear our pleas for your help in our time of need. We beg you to come to our assistance. We beg you to use your mighty strength to make Qwunus, that angry orca, go away from the mouth of our salmon river.

Saghalie Tyee, Great Spirit, guide the mighty Thunderbird, make him understand how much we need his help, before the People of the Salmon are no more. You who gave us the salmon know how it sustains us in every season, even through the winter months when the salmon return to their village under the ocean. Do not forsake us, your people.

Come mighty Thunderbird, come and drive away the greedy one, we pray to you."

All through the night, Golden Eye and the

council in the sweat lodge chanted and prayed. Their focus was very intense. Golden Eye could feel the strength of their spirits as they all joined in this most important task. From time to time he felt all their spirits come together and rush to the mighty Thunderbird. Golden Eye thought he could feel the impact of their spirits on the Thunderbird; feel the giant bird rise up in his lair, ruffling his feathers and glancing about, causing lightning bolts to fly from his eyes and thunder to roll as he flapped his wings.

"Time to go," said Golden Eye. "He's coming."

Just before dawn, they exited the sweat lodge and pulled their capes about their shoulders in the chill, damp air. A few crickets and frogs still called their night songs and the first sleepy robin gave out a tentative chirrup. Dew was heavy on the grass and a quarter moon slid in and out of misty clouds. The men went to the longhouses and woke the villagers up.

"Come, everyone. Let us go up onto the high hill and watch. Let's see if Thunderbird answers our prayers." Sleeping babies were strapped into their carrying packs, toddlers nestled into their mother and fathers' shoulders, and the whole village traipsed sleepily up to the high ground.

The crowd stood in absolute silence, waiting. A few minutes later, the first streaks of dawn lightened the sky. The dawn wind blew, brushing their hair back and causing them to draw in lungfuls of the fresh morning air. As the sun began to crest the horizon, they were able to see the huge orca at the lower reach of the river, filling the river, shore to shore. It charged at the shoals of salmon, whose instincts told them they must get up that river to their home.

Then, from above and behind the crowd came the most bone-chilling scream the people had ever heard and a massive shadow passed over them as Thunderbird flew by, aiming for Qwunus, the orca. Thunderbird was so large that the flapping of his wings made arbutus trees near the river bend down, caused the big, heavy canoes on the beach to roll over and the people to fall flat on the ground. His body was as big as a longhouse, each feather the size of a small child, and his eyes did indeed flash lightning bolts, most of them directed at the killer whale.

Qwunus, distracted from the salmon by the horrendous scream of Thunderbird and by the lightning bolts that boiled the water around him, turned to face this disturbance. As he turned, Thunderbird wheeled and brought down his legs that were like trees and his giant claws with their viciously curved talons. He drove those talons into the sides of the orca, just ahead of his tall, black dorsal fin and lifted the orca, who must have weighed as much as two hundred men, out of the water.

Thunderbird flapped his great wings and carried the orca toward land but the whale overcame his shock

and reacted. He twisted and arched so strongly that Thunderbird lost his grip and the whale dropped with a thunderous splash back into the river. Thunderbird swept over the watching crowd of villagers, the wind from his wings knocking them all to the ground again. He rose to a great height, whirled and then, with an ear-splitting scream, dove at the killer whale and snatched him up again, his mighty talons sunk deep into Qwunus's sides. The whale twisted and bucked with all his might, letting out a high-pitched scream.

Thunderbird carried the whale away from the water until they were above the flat land to the east of the village where he dropped the orca, from a height above the tallest trees. The killer whale landed with an earth-shaking thud and in a moment, Thunderbird was once again upon him. Qwunus writhed and flipped and did his best to bite Thunderbird with his massive mouthful of teeth but he was like a fish out of water, out of his element. Though the battle raged on between the two great beasts with blood and feathers spraying all over the area, Qwunus, the supernatural orca, was doomed.

When Thunderbird finally knew that the killer whale was finished, he rose into the air and gave an incredibly loud scream of victory. Then he zoomed away to his nest with a large chunk of orca flesh in his beak to share with his family.

The people of the Qu'wutsun village stood in

shock. Never had even the oldest of them witnessed any battle so wild, so vicious. Now the silence, after all that horrendous noise, was almost deafening. After a while though, with the orca not moving but oozing his lifeblood onto the plain, a few curious and hungry dogs wandered tentatively over to sniff the carcass.

This brought the people back to action and they all scrambled down the hill and went to inspect that which had been causing them so much grief. Before anyone touched it though, the bent and wrinkled old shaman delivered a heart-felt prayer of thanks to the Thunderbird and to the Great Spirit for their deliverance. Once again, the People of the Salmon would have as many salmon as they needed, for now and for the wintertime. Indeed, as they looked at the river, they saw salmon virtually swarming up the river.

"Look at that," yelled one of the men, "I bet you could walk right across the river on their backs, there's so many of them!"

Everyone laughed and hollered back and forth in joy. Right away, some of the men set off to tend the upstream weirs so that they didn't become clogged with the massive surge of salmon. When they had all they could use for now, they would open up the weirs so that they wouldn't be destroyed by the sheer number of salmon trying to pass through. Other men went to get their carving tools to cut up the meat of the killer whale – no need to let it go to waste – but when they returned to the site of the battle, there was nothing left but the bloodied ground. It had indeed been a supernatural beast and had returned to the spirit world.

The women and girls busied themselves preparing the morning meal because even after that astounding battle life had to go on and breakfast had to be prepared as always. A gentle breeze rustled in the branches of the trees: the pines, the cedars, the alder and arbutus as dry leaves skittered across the clearing. Birds sang again and the sun, now high in the sky, sent waves of warmth down on the people and the land.

After a breakfast of very fresh salmon, Golden Eye and the other night-long chanters found a quiet place to get some welcome sleep. The others of the village carried on catching, cleaning and smoking the bumper crop of salmon. Tan Buck worked shoulder to shoulder with the men and boys until near sunset. A quick swim and scrub-down in the river left them tingling and refreshed and ready for the evening meal for sure, and what a dinner it was! Boiled salmon, baked salmon, steamed salmon; smoked salmon, even salmon roe eggs, with side dishes of steamed seaweed and roasted potato-like camas bulbs. There were fresh huckleberries for dessert and all was washed down with gallons of salal tea and spring water – a feast fit for the Great Spirit himself! Then everyone settled back and waited for story time to begin.

Chapter Four

Stones and Stoneheads

"We noticed a number of really big, strange-looking rocks on our way here," Tan Buck observed.

"Yes, we recognized the boulders that Sum-ul-quatz used to crush old Shu-shu-cum at Sansum Narrows," chimed in Golden Eye, "but what about all those others? Do you know how they came to be there?"

"Ah, yes, you have good sharp eyes," exclaimed the old man, Ocean Traveler, former head shaman of the village. "Long ago, before our grandfathers' time, the Great Spirit came down in the form of a man called Heels to check up on the humans and see if they were behaving themselves. He rewarded those who were good and punished those who were not. The deer of the forest are the result of Heels meeting with a man who was making arrowheads from sharpened seashells with which to shoot Heels when he came by. That man was obviously guilty of something bad, so Heels stuck those sharp shells into the man's head and turned him into a deer, telling him to leap away into the forest and that forever, deer would be eaten by man.

Up there on that hill, if you walk through the brush, you will find an upright stone that was a man who was running to hide from Heels. Heh, heh, heh…..he didn't make it, did he?

Down the river there, do you see a rock that looks like a crouching man and in the water a long, flat rock? That is where Heels caught a man spying on a woman who was swimming. Turned them both to stone. Further down the river you will see his canoe and the post he tied it to – turned to stone as well.

One evildoer he turned into the moose by clapping broad pieces of wood onto the sides of his head then sending him into the swamp to eat grass for all time.

Far up the river, Kissach, the Great Chief of the Quamichan, got into a staring contest with Heels. Kissach lost and finally walked into the lake there and became a stony reminder of the power of the Great Spirit. While Heels was there he turned the dancing sunlight on the surface of the lake into trout and sent them swimming in the lake and down the river for good people to enjoy.

Along his way he also helped people, teaching them how to make use of the bounty of the field, forest and water, and showed them how to use flint and rock friction to make fire. Where would we be without that, eh?"

"Was that Kissach the same one who fought the bullies of the Stonehead People?" queried Tree Moss, a pretty girl of ten summers.

"It was indeed," replied Thunder Cloud, the Great Chief's brother. "I remember that story being told to me when I was young like you."

"Tell it to us, tell it to us!" came a chorus of young voices.

"Very well," said Thunder Cloud. "Kissach's grandmother had been stolen from here by the horrible Stonehead people from the south. They were called Stoneheads because they couldn't be killed by ordinary means. Arrows bounced off them and war clubs shattered on contact with their heads. So our ancestors learned to steer clear of them. But, like I said, one of our beautiful young women was stolen by the Stoneheads. Their chief was fascinated by her and so she was not beaten or starved. He even made her his third wife.

By and by she gave birth to a daughter, a child who grew to be even more beautiful than her mother. All the young men wanted to marry her and brought her father many gifts so he would choose one of them for her husband. The chief said that she must decide for herself. She didn't choose any of those young men. In fact, one day she was out gathering grasses for weaving when she saw a young man of our village standing in the edge of the forest with his hand raised in greeting. He was handsome and strong and many of our girls wanted him as a husband but he thought they were too silly. These two talked all day and met again and again until finally she told her father that she had chosen this young man as her husband.

The chief agreed, but only if the young man would live there so that there would be peace with our people. A great potlatch was held and the young couple was married and settled in. Unfortunately, the chief showed so much favour to that young man that others became jealous and tried to kill him, even having the medicine man create an evil spell. However, the spell was misdirected and killed the chief himself! Well, things went from bad to worse for the young couple and one day, the young man was killed by the Stonehead men, something they would never have dared to do if the chief had been alive to protect him.

The young woman was pregnant at the time and when her baby was about to be born, the first wives and the medicine men conspired to kill the baby. The girl suspected this and fended off their offers to help with the birth. She gave birth secretly, then escaped into the forest with her newborn son, Kissach. She raised Kissach in the forest and as he grew, he displayed great strength and wisdom and even some magical powers, like talking to birds, who warned him of dangers. He loved to hear about his father but she didn't tell him of how his father died, waiting until he was older. By the age of six summers, he was adept with a bow and arrow and brought home many birds for food. His mother saved all of the wings and skins of these birds.

By the age of fourteen summers he was bringing home large animals. At seventeen summers, he brought down a really big elk buck, made a travois and carted it home where his mother made a fine covering from the hide and many tools from the bones. While bathing he scrubbed himself with fir bark which made his skin bleed. When he threw the bark into the water, the blood drops turned into a mass of trout.

At eighteen summers, she finally told him how his father had died. Kissach was enraged and swore revenge on the Stonehead warriors. His mother warned him that he would not be able to kill them by ordinary means. She had been thinking all through the years of what she would do when this moment came. She told him that he must learn to fly and to find a club that would not shatter on stone. She had secretly made him a cape of all the bird wings and skins that he had brought home over the years. She put this cape around him and took him up to the waterfall there, up the river. There she taught him to jump off and glide into the meadow. Kissach himself searched and searched for a war club that would not shatter and finally he found a knot of a yew tree that would actually shatter rocks!

So, at the next full moon, he crept along the ridge of that mountain to the south of us. He saw the Stonehead warriors engaged in a game with a woven ball and he swooped down over them. He challenged them but they all fled home in terror. He returned another day with several yew clubs and this time the Stoneheads weren't afraid. They called out 'Come birdman, we are ready with our arrows.' Kissach glided over the group, swinging his club and killing three of them. On his next leap he killed even more, then he chased the rest of them and felled them too, yelling out 'For my father!' The lone survivor of the Stoneheads escaped and fled up to the Nanaimo people and he told them the story.

Kissach and his mother took possession of the Stonehead village and he became a mighty chief, much loved by the people for his fairness and goodness. He taught all the young boys his skills and trained them in ways of wisdom. Other tribes paid him honour too, bringing many gifts of furs, blankets and food as thanks for ridding the area of the Stoneheads and bringing peace to our valley. One of the greatest potlatches ever was held in his honour. If you listen carefully, on still nights you can still hear the echoes of that great celebration."

All the young faces stared up at Thunder

Cloud's face in wonder, Golden Eye and Tan Buck among them. Golden Eye, a lover of fine stories who longed to be a great storyteller himself, felt a great sense of kinship with Kissach plus a great sense of the history of the region settling around him, like a blanket.

Just then Big Head reached for a water-filled

bladder, knocked it over, tried to grab it and ended up spraying water all over everyone near him. Children and adults jumped up and scattered, more to get out of the way of his flying legs and arms than the water. People shouted and laughed while some of the young men helped Big Head up, brushing dirt and twigs off him, passing him another water pouch so he could actually have a drink.

The fire was dying down by then so the adults decided it was time they and the little children should go off to sleep. The young people, aged ten to twenty summers, threw another log on the fire and sat up for a while longer, talking, listening to the fire crackle and gazing up at the countless millions of stars overhead. The sight of those stars reminded Golden Eye of a story.

"Have you heard the story Red Eye, White Eye?" he asked.

"No," cried some of the younger people, "tell it to us!"

The older ones had heard the story but they just smiled and settled in to hear it again. It was a favourite of theirs too.

"Long ago, when the world was different from today and the stars were closer to the land, two brothers of sixteen and eighteen summers were sitting around their fire when they saw two holes in the sky with just one red star and one white star in them. They wondered about those holes and they thought that maybe there were people up there, looking down on them.

'Maybe they are pretty girls who want to meet us,' said the older boy wishfully.

'But how can we get up there?' wondered the younger boy.

'Well, you're the best runner and swimmer, but I am the best with a bow and arrow. How about if I shoot arrows up there, one into the bottom of the other until they reach from here to there? Then I'll climb up there and check things out.'

The younger brother begged and pleaded to be allowed to go up the arrow ladder too but his brother said no.

'You stay here and come in the canoe when I call. I will call so loudly from up there that all the babies will cry and the dogs will bark so you will know I am ready to come down.'

Three weeks later, when there was just a sliver of a moon, the older brother did as he had said - climbed up the arrows and was soon in the land above the stars. The people there seemed much the same but the trees and the birds were very strange, with weird shapes and colours. As he walked along, the young man met a very old woman who stopped him and warned him that he should go back home immediately, that there was great danger here. The young man asked her to tell of the danger and how he might protect himself because he was determined to stay and find the girls who had been watching him and his brother. The old woman shrugged and said that he must find three things to protect himself: a bird skin, an octopus, and a clam shell with fine white powder in it.

'Thank you, grandmother,' said the young man. 'How will these protect me?'

'There is an evil woman up ahead. If she catches you alone you are doomed and will never be seen again. But if she should catch you, breathe in some of the white powder and you will become so small that you will fit into the bird skin and fly away from her. Take another pinch of the powder and you will be your own size again but don't ever drop the powder or it will cause a huge explosion!'

'What about the octopus?' the young man asked.

'The girls you seek, Red Eye and White Eye, play by that lake by day and then by night they peek down on the earth. You must use the powder to change into the octopus and swim with the girls, letting them get to know you.'

With that, she wished him well and began to walk away down the path. Then she turned.

'Beware of the girls' father!' she called as her last warning.

The young man carried on and he saw many strange things such as a running frog and trees with blue leaves! He found for himself the three things the old woman had recommended and took them along with him. Soon after he came upon a woman who was crying because she had dropped her ring. The young man offered to help.

'My eyes are too dim to see it, but follow its brightness and you will find it,' she cried.

As he looked about, the young man saw one of the blue-leaved trees split open. As he bent to look inside he saw the ring there but the evil woman pushed him into the tree and it snapped shut!

'Ha, ha!' she cackled, 'I have destroyed many this way. Now again there is one less to come after our young women.'

Caught in the midst of the tree, the young man remembered what the old woman had said. He sniffed a little of the white powder and became tiny. He slipped on the bird skin and flew up, pecked out a knothole and escaped from the blue-leafed tree.

He flew off down the trail and soon came to the lake where Red Eye and White Eye were playing and splashing in the water. The young man sniffed a little more of the powder and turned himself into an octopus. He swam about near the girls and actually reached out and touched one of them on the leg.

'How nasty!' screamed Red Eye

'I think he's nice'" said White Eye and she picked him up and petted him.

'Throw him away before he kills you!' cried Red Eye, scrubbing her back with a red sponge.

The young man sniffed some powder, changed back into himself and stood on the shore of the lake. The two sisters wrapped themselves in soft mantles. They had never seen anyone like him before.

'I am a stranger from the world below the stars. I saw you looking down at night and came up here to meet you.'

Red Eye, not trusting the boy, planned to get him to their home so their father could finish him off. 'Welcome,' she said. 'Come and meet our father, he will be glad to see you.'

The young man remembered the old woman's warning but went along and climbed up to their home.

'You may have the hand of Red Eye in marriage,' said the father, a massive, frightening-looking man.

'Thank you but I would rather have White Eye, if you please,' replied the young man.

'No! Red Eye is the eldest. She must marry first!' screamed the father.

'I have special ways to end your seeking,' crooned Red Eye, with evil lurking in her heart.

'No. I will have White Eye and no other,' demanded the young man.

Then, while the father and Red Eye were immobilized with rage, the young man grabbed up White Eye and rushed off with her. Seeing that Red Eye and her father were about to chase after him, the young man flung the clamshell into the house. The clamshell exploded and blew up the house, killing the evil father and Red Eye. The smoke from that fire has ever since darkened that red star so that now it only glows dimly.

The young man of eighteen summers ran with White Eye to the top of the arrow ladder and called out in a mighty voice for his brother of sixteen summers. The younger brother heard what he thought was a loud rumble of thunder that made the dogs bark and the babies cry. Then he heard his brother's voice yelling 'Come' so he jumped in his canoe and paddled to the arrow ladder in time to see his brother and White Eye descend.

And so, the young brave and White Eye came safely down to earth at Q'uwutsun Bay and lived happily for many years. White Eye returned to the heavens when she died and now when we look up at the stars, we can see the dull glow of Red Eye but White Eye is the bright, clear evening star. It was the first star to cease to flicker and has ever since been a steady light."

The eyes of the young girls in the circle around the fire shone in enjoyment of the romantic story. The young boys' and men's eyes reflected the joy of the adventure and triumph of their long-ago ancestors.

"Well, that's definitely enough for tonight," chimed in Big Head. "We growing boys need our sleep."

To a chorus of laughter, the young people got up and made their way to their beds, anticipating happy dreams. Golden Eye lay awake for a while, his mind in a whirl. So much had happened already since he and Tan Buck had left home.

"Hey, are you asleep?" whispered Tan Buck.

"Not yet," Golden Eye whispered back.

"What a day that was! I'm so tired I can't fall asleep."

"I know, I can't either."

"Are we leaving tomorrow?"

"I think we'd better. We have a long way to go and we want to be back home before winter."

"You have a lot further to go than I do," yawned Tan Buck as his voice trailed off.

"Right, let's try to get some sleep."

Crickets and tree frogs sang their nocturnal chorus and the boys were drifting off when they suddenly heard a high-pitched scream and a frightening snarl, then silence.

"Sounds like that Killer Cat just grabbed himself a rabbit for a midnight meal," murmured Big Head sleepily.

Golden Eye and Tan Buck snuggled deeper under their blankets, hearts pounding, and only their tiredness let them sink into slumber.

Chapter Five

On to Adventure

The next morning, after bathing and eating another meal of fresh salmon, Golden Eye and Tan Buck said their goodbyes and their thanks to the people of Big Head's village and headed off. Big Head accompanied them back to the ocean shore, carrying with him a bladder of fresh spring water and a pouch of smoked salmon for the boys' journey.

"I wish I was going with you, but we're so far behind with salmon drying for winter that they need me here."

"We know. Thank you anyway, Big Head; it's been great being here. Thank you for everything and watch out for low branches!" teased Golden Eye.

"See you on the way back!" yelled Tan Buck as they pushed off and paddled away, singing the paddling song.

The morning was glorious. The sun was rising

above the mountains on the Great Land, seagulls wheeled and called in their raucous voices and all the other birds sang their morning songs. The boys had left a dark trail through the dew-wet grass and there was a definite chill to the early morning air. It was, after all, the time of the ninth moon and certainly no longer summer. More and more dry leaves fell each day.

Golden Eye was feeling quietly happy as his paddling muscles began stretching and working. He was glad to be on his way again; glad to have Tan Buck paddling behind him. He was feeling somewhat older - more grown up these days. He searched his mind for the source of this feeling and decided that his eyes were wider open to the adult world. He had been welcomed into the elders' sweat lodge and had been trusted to use his spirit powers to assist the shamans of his own village and the village on Protector Island.

"Responsibility," he thought, "I've taken and been given responsibility and I have to live up to the trust that has been placed in me."

Still, he was having fun, just like he did when he was a child. He was looking forward to his journey and meeting the people of the great whaling nation. So what if he would be alone on the journey west? He was young and strong, skilled with bow and knife, AND protected by the spirits. How could he lose?

"Look up ahead," called out Tan Buck.

The boys had been paddling for several hours,

delighting in the sight of all the many-shaped bays and towering headlands, the green valleys and splashing streams plus the small rivers that ran out to this, the eastern shore of Protector Island. Now they were coming to the mouth of a really large river and there on the shore stood a boy of about their age. He too was barefoot and wearing just a short garment tied around his waist. He had a small fire burning on the beach and he waved to Golden Eye and Tan Buck.

"That must be your Kwakwaka'wakw guide, Tan Buck," said Golden Eye, "come to lead you to their village up at the north end of Protector Island."

"Yes, I think so," echoed Tan Buck over the noise of the great river. "Look at all the salmon going up!"

"I know, I've never seen so many in one river, or such a big river either!" yelled Golden Eye.

The boys brought their canoe up to the beach, jumping out before it could be scraped too much on the rocks. They carefully lifted it out of the water and then turned to greet the other lad.

"Kla-how-eya, Tillicum," offered Tan Buck. "Hello, friend."

"Gilakasla," said the boy. "I am Swims-With-Seals. You are the Salish boy I am to lead to my village?"

Golden Eye and Tan Buck stole a quick look at each other. They were aware of what the boy was saying but somehow he sounded different – some of his Kwak'wala words were a little unfamiliar. Thinking back to potlatches of the past, the boys adjusted their ears and knew to just keep talking. Using the Chinook trading words from their uncles, the meaning of their sentences would be understood. Words like peshak, meaning bad, mahka - go away or get out, mahse mahse - thank you, kleshe - good; wau wau meaning talk or speak, mamook - work, hyas till - very heavy and mesika meaning yours helped the conversation along.

Swims-With-Seals also looked a little different, slightly taller, slimmer, and shorter of arm. There was a bit of a difference to his facial bone structure – a little more finely featured but with a slight hook to his nose.

"Yes, I am Tan Buck and this is my friend, Golden Eye."

"Welcome Tan Buck and Golden Eye. My village will be very grateful to you, Tan Buck, for the return of my uncle's bones so that he may rest with his ancestors. We have also heard of you, Golden Eye. Is it true that you swim with the killer whales?"

"Well, I swim with ONE killer whale - my friend Black Fin. He sort of adopted me one day and boy am I glad he picked that day. He also attacked someone who was trying to kill me – kill us – and saved us both."

"And you have been on your vision quest

already and are protected by the Wolf Spirit? I see that you carry a wolf skin."

"Yes. This is all that remains of Old One Eye, my companion and protector since I was a baby. I guess he knew even way back then that my spirit was kindred to the wolves."

"That is a fine pelt. It will be good to rest upon or to cover yourself on colder nights. I hear that you are going to visit the Nootka people. We sometimes travel around the north end of Protector Island and down the western shore to visit them, when the Western Ocean is calm, that is."

"Well, I guess I'll see it for myself soon. I have had dreams of being with them and so I think I am being drawn there. You will take care of my headstrong friend here, won't you? He is a fine spirit dancer and a good, strong, loyal friend but he tends to act first and think later so I'm always getting him out of trouble."

Tan Buck gave Golden Eye a friendly shove.

"Get on your way, big mouth," he said. "Go see the giant whales and their slayers. Swims-With-Seals and I will take good care of your canoe 'til you come to the Kwakwaka'wakw village in the next moon, won't we?"

"Indeed we will. Now Golden Eye, follow this river to the long lake. Take the canoe and go all the way to the other end, then follow the streams westward and beyond the caves a long inlet will take you down to the Nootka village. Goodbye and may the good spirits be with you."

"Goodbye Golden Eye. Be careful in the woods. See you soon," said Tan Buck as he and Swims-With-Seals launched the canoe and headed North.

"Watch out for the yai, the little supernatural people and for Dzunuk'wa, The-Wild-Woman-of-the-Forest-Who-Eats-Children," yelled Swims-With-Seals.

"I'm not a child! Goodbye. Take care of yourselves and have a pleasant journey," Golden Eye called after them.

Golden Eye watched them paddle away with mixed feelings. There went his canoe, on which he had relied for rapid transportation for the past year and there went his best friend with someone else. He also felt alone again, a chilly feeling inside. He was nowhere near his family or anyone of his village for the first time in his life. He searched his spirit and felt the connections: with his big, strong father, his gentle mother and wise grandmother, plus the powerful spirit of his shaman grandfather.

'I am with you,' came the feeling from his grandfather.

Golden Eye felt reassured, reconnected, and he turned and sat on a rock by the fire to eat and drink before heading off up the river. A short way off he noticed a ring-tailed raccoon washing his own meal at the edge of the river. It turned its masked face toward Golden Eye, made a churring sound, and returned to its meal.

"You'd make a wonderful pillow with that fat rump of yours and your lovely soft fur with no smell to it," said Golden Eye softly. "However, I know you like to be up most of the night so you just wouldn't be available would you, even if you were willing?"

Golden Eye chuckled to himself as he watched the raccoon waddle-run up to a pine tree and scurry up it. The raccoon made himself a bed where four branches jutted out, as with all pine trees, in a circle around the trunk.

"I'll keep that in mind," thought Golden Eye. "I haven't had to sleep in a tree yet but you never know."

He splashed some water on the campfire and spread the coals to cool. He slung his tied-up wolf-skin over his shoulder and checked his small pouches of food, water and medicines. He took one last look at the ocean, the islands and the Great Land, then struck off inland, following the great salmon river. Remembering the story of the First Brothers, Golden Eye bathed in the river before he set off. He too wanted to increase his strength with the spirit world.

The loud rushing noise of the river and the splashing of the salmon as they swam mightily against the strong downstream current on their way to their spawning grounds kept Golden Eye headed in the right direction. He began to enjoy the coolness of the forest that grew so thickly here. Some of the trees, the great firs and cedars, even had moss dripping from their branches.

Before too long, Golden Eye came to a smaller river leading off to his left. He took the opportunity to bathe in it too. As he was drying off with some tree moss he heard, above the flow of the small river and even that of the great salmon river, what sounded like a waterfall. Curious, he trekked a short way along the smaller river and, as it bent to the right, Golden Eye did indeed see a really tall waterfall in the not-too-far distance. Could this be the waterfall that he had heard about at Big Head's village – the one that might have a spirit within it? He had to find out. Checking that the sun was still well before the mid-afternoon mark, he figured he had time for a short detour. He set off at as fast a pace as he could while negotiating the boulders and overhanging tree trunks along the river.

Chapter Six

Killer Cat and The Waterfall Spirit

Several hundred paces along the way, Golden Eye got a strange feeling; like someone or something was watching him. Instinctively, he stepped beside the trunk of a nearby cedar tree. As he moved, he felt something brush his left shoulder. In a split second he got behind the tree and swiveled around to see what it was. He found himself staring into the eyes of the Killer Cat, a full-grown mountain lion. For a moment boy and cat were frozen, sucked into the vortex of each other's eyes, taking each other's measure, determining the possibilities of the situation, deciding whether to flee or fight.

Golden Eye realized the immense power of the cat's bulging muscles, the size of the claw-hiding paws, the viciousness in its eyes, and decided to spring up into the tree. He grabbed the lowest branch and quickly hauled himself up onto it, then scrambled around the tree through the branches to keep the big cat in view. The cat, surprised at Golden Eye's move, crouched and prepared to leap into the tree himself; the same tree from which he had launched himself so silently at his supposed prey, Golden Eye.

Before the cat could leap, however, Golden Eye was inspired to draw about himself the pelt and head of his old wolf-friend. Leaning forward and down toward the cat, he presented the astounding aspect of a wolf

about to leap from a tree! This move so shocked the cat that he recoiled, spun around and crashed off into the forest.

Golden Eye sat back on the sturdy branch and caught his breath for a few moments. His mind finally began to think, not just react, and he thought about not only the great size of the beast - as large as Golden Eye's father - twice as long if you considered the black-tipped tail. The fury in the cat's yellow, pointed oval eyes in its not-so-large head, its rounded triangular ears, the stark white muzzle of fur surrounding its mouth beneath its broad flat nose, all settled into Golden Eye's consciousness. What had impressed him most, however, was the sinewy strength of the muscles rippling beneath its tawny, reddish-beige fur and white belly. He admired the agility of the beast as it twisted and lithely manoeuvered over and around the standing and fallen trees as it vanished into the underbrush.

"Well, what should I do now?" Golden Eye wondered out loud to himself. "Carry on to the waterfall or head back to the salmon river?"

His mind quickly ran over the time of day, the nearness of the mountain lion and the draw of the waterfall. The waterfall won and he swung down from the tree, gave it a pat of thanks for its protection and struck off toward the sound of the falling water. Golden Eye made his way through a thick stand of fir trees, keeping the river on his right side. The nearer he got to the waterfall though, the louder its noise. As the forest became thinner, the terrain became filled with water-loving ferns, ending where jumbled clusters of rocks piled up around the pool below the falls.

Golden Eye gazed up at the waterfall as spray from it coated his face, hair and body. The falls were about forty steps wide at their top, high above him, perhaps two hundred steps up. The water falling down toward Golden Eye seemed to be floating, free-falling, if he looked at just one spot of it. Yet, taken altogether it seemed to be a speeding torrent, crashing into the pool at its bottom and raising a vaporous cloud there before settling and running off down the little river.

Halfway up the waterfall, Golden Eye saw a flat ledge of rock just to the right of the streaming water.

"Should I try for that?" he wondered.

Before the thought had finished forming itself, Golden Eye felt himself being propelled, flattened, into the pool. The Killer Cat was upon him, his fangs aiming for Golden Eye's throat! Golden Eye rolled quickly onto his back, bringing his knees and his elbows forward, trying to create a space between his body and that of the mountain lion. This rolling motion caused the cat's huge right paw to come down upon a rock made slippery by wet moss and he momentarily lost his balance.

Golden Eye took immediate advantage of this

and shoved himself backward, out from under the cat, into the deeper water of the pool. He flung his wolf pelt away as he moved. The great cat recovered his balance and sprang, screaming horribly at Golden Eye. Golden Eye rolled to his right and dove down into the pool as the cat's claws scratched the back of his head and his shoulders.

Down and down Golden Eye swam, slowly expelling the big breath he had gulped before

submerging. The Killer Cat swam down too, but, out of his natural element, he surfaced before long and climbed out onto the rocks beside the pool, awaiting his next chance to attack.

Golden Eye opened his eyes underwater and noticed the turbulence of the water at the bottom of the falls. He headed for it. He swam with a strong breast-stroke and powerful kicks of his legs until he touched the wall of rock behind the waterfall. He surfaced there, catching a breath with his face up against the rock wall but quickly realized that he couldn't stay there long. The force of the down-rushing water was even then forcing him down and away from the rock wall, propelling him toward the pool and the snarling beast awaiting him there. Golden Eye could see that the cat was aware of him there and was making its way over the jumbled rocks toward the side of the falls.

Golden Eye knew that he was no real match for those jaws and claws on level ground. He decided it was time to connect with Grandfather Strong Oak's spirit and escape by spirit magic. He launched himself out through the waterfall toward the opposite shore from the Killer Cat. Once again the force of the waterfall pushed him under the surface of the pool. With a great snarl, the cat leapt into the water, swimming with powerful strokes toward where Golden Eye would come up.

Imagine the cat's amazement when a bird, not a

boy, erupted from the water and flapped up to the high ledge where it perched, fluttered off the water, and turned back into Golden Eye.  The Killer Cat's eyes, despite his shock, had followed the bird-that-was-Golden Eye to his landing spot. He spun in the water, hauled himself out and searched for a route up to the bird-boy.

Golden Eye, in the meantime, saw that the ledge extended behind the waterfall and he made his way through the thick spray to where the water arced away from the rock face. Not only was there a ledge, there was even an indentation in the rock wall and here Golden Eye sat down to rest. He could neither see nor hear the mountain lion and felt he was safe for the time being. He took some time to catch his breath and sort out his feelings.

"Why," he wondered, "is this big cat chasing me?" The elders of Big Head's village had told him that it was rare for a mountain lion to hunt or kill a human, but not unheard of. Perhaps some person had offended this cat – stolen its kill, injured it, or trapped it – and the cat had decided that all humans were its enemies. Whatever was the case, it was now on Golden Eye's trail and meant to harm him.

Golden Eye thought this through. He did not

have any reason to hate the beautiful beast. In fact he admired its speed and agility, its cleverness and its beauty.

"I'll just have to avoid him," he thought, "if at all possible."

Remembering how good it was to have had Old One Eye, the wolf, following him and protecting him all through his life, he couldn't bring himself to hate an animal simply because it was big and strong and scary. It was just another creature of the earth with just as much right to exist as he had himself. However, Golden Eye had to protect and defend himself too, so that he continued to exist as well. He also realized, with a shiver, that he was alone on this trail. The trail! He had to get back on the trail toward the Nootka people.

"How long will it be until that big cat goes away and forgets about having me for its dinner?" he wondered out loud.

"Perhaps you should send your thoughts somewhere else to confuse him," came a voice near Golden Eye's shoulder.

Golden Eye jumped, caught himself just in time so that he didn't tumble out into the falls and twisted his head around, back and forth to see where the voice had come from. Finally he looked directly into the falling water and there was the face of a woman! It was the same face he had seen in the clouds when he was three summers old and threw his spirit into the sky. He had seen her face in the beaver pond in which he could have drowned when he was only one summer old. He saw her again while he was canoeing with Tan Buck last summer, and also in the smoke of his fire on his vision quest.

"Hello," Golden Eye said in a shaky voice. "Who are you?"

"I am Wolf Woman." she replied.

Golden Eye looked more closely and saw that

Wolf Woman was indeed a spirit, transparent, not a human being. Her face was beautiful. Her eyes carried wisdom, understanding and kindness. Her long hair floated about in the water and she seemed to be robed in a blanket that was either fringed with hair or else tattered with age. It was difficult to tell in the midst of the waterfall. Golden Eye was amazed but kept his wits about himself, realizing that this was his first opportunity to actually speak with his 'Lady-in-the-Water'. Also, perhaps she could advise him how to get out of this situation!

"Welcome, Wolf Woman. I am very happy to meet you at last. Have you been watching over me all my life?"

"I, as a representative of the Wolf Spirits, have been appointed to watch you grow and to assist in small ways when it is necessary."

"I am most grateful for your protection and guidance," said Golden Eye, in a humble tone.

His mind was reeling. In the past few minutes he had been attacked by an angry mountain lion, had to fight for his life, swam beneath a waterfall, turned into a bird, found a secret ledge behind the waterfall and now was talking to a spirit! This spirit, whose face he had been seeing all his life, was now actually speaking to him though; a very comforting fact.

"It is wonderful to see you again, and especially to hear you. I feel so alone here and my mind has not been clear for the last few minutes. I could really use some advice just now. Do you have any for me?"

"I am here just to help you focus. You have inside you all the resources you need to succeed in your journey. You know that the big cat that is following you will lose your scent with all this water between you and soon he will have to go off to find food. So, just rest a little while and then get back on the path toward the Western Ocean. Remember to stay in touch with your senses. Use all the lessons from your childhood. Call upon the Great Spirit and your wolf protector spirits for strength and you'll be fine. I go now. Another awaits you near your journey's end. Farewell, Golden Eye. Remember to use your own powers as much as possible, relying on spirit power only when you must."

Wolf Woman's image faded into the falling curtain of water and Golden Eye felt a shiver of chill pass through him. He took a moment to focus and gather his wits then crept back along the ledge to the edge of the waterfall. He peered out, examined the brush near him, looked up higher and then down toward the pool at the bottom of the falls. The big cat was not to be seen so he cautiously stepped out, stood still and listened and carefully scanned every possible place it might be hiding. He saw nothing unnatural and heard nothing but the roar of the waterfall. Golden Eye took a deep, grateful breath and scrambled down to the pool at the bottom of the falls. He was gathering up his wolf skin when he noticed something. Right beside where the wolf skin had lain was a scraped together pile of leaves, soaked in strong-smelling urine.

"All right, big cat, I get your message. This is your territory, not mine. I'm just passing through so goodbye."

Golden Eye made a cup of his hand and took a refreshing drink of water from the pool, then he stood up, brushed his hair back from his face and took off at a jog. He retraced his path along the small river back to the big salmon river. With a renewed sense of purpose and determination he forged off toward the Western Ocean and the people of the great whaling nation. With every step he took, however, he kept his eyes and ears on high alert for signs of the big cat.

Chapter Seven

My Meal, Your Meal, Help!

Golden Eye looked up. He had been following along the great salmon river for some time and he was checking the position of the sun to see how many hours of traveling time he had left. The sun was ahead of him. Since he was traveling westward, in the same direction as the sun's daily journey, and since it was the time of the ninth moon, he knew that he would have fewer hours of daylight to travel than during the sixth moon. He wanted to make as much progress as possible before dark.

In the trees around him, families of birds kept up a chattering chorus as he passed: chickadees, red-breasted nuthatches, band-tailed pigeons and the noisy, cheeky stellar jays who liked to mimic other birds. One was pretending to be a hawk but his brilliant blue and grey colouring gave him away. Tiny wrens flitted about in the undergrowth and a fat ruffed grouse perched on a low branch. Golden Eye's stomach rumbled with hunger so he bent and picked up a sharp, solid stone and said a small prayer asking the grouse to give himself as food. He slowly stood up and whizzed the stone straight and true, knocking the grouse out of the tree.

"Thank you, friend grouse," he said.

Golden Eye tipped his flint rock and striking stone out of one of the pouches around his neck and within minutes had a small fire going. While the larger sticks began to burn, Golden Eye cleaned the stinking entrails out, then defeathered the grouse and skewered it on a sturdy stick. He pushed the stick into the ground at an angle so that the meat of the bird was just above the flames.

It took just a few minutes to cook as he turned the stick around and around. When clear juices dripped into the fire, he knew it was ready. He pulled the stick out of the ground and, after blowing and waving it around a bit, sat down by his fire and enjoyed his small feast.

While he ate he had burned all the feathers and entrails and when he had finished he put out the small fire with dirt. He took a quick, refreshing dip in the river and brought back some water to pour on the fire site. He left little evidence that he had even been there; nothing but a wisp of fire smoke and the scent of the succulent meat.

So, refreshed and strengthened, Golden Eye pressed on. He kept the sound of the river on his right as he made his way because sometimes a tangle of trees or a huge rock formation forced him to move inland and find a way ahead through easier terrain. It was on one of these diversions away from the river that Golden Eye saw a wondrous sight! He was on a flat plain, from which green, rolling hills spread up toward the central island mountain range. One mountaintop stood high above the others and bore snow on its peak. "Is that snow from last winter," Golden Eye wondered, "or has there been an early snow here, that high up?"

As he watched the sun glance off the snowy peak, Golden Eye heard a strange, rumbling sound. He turned to his left and his eyes could hardly believe what they saw. Rushing toward the hills came a herd of animals. But what were they? They looked something like deer but they were much bigger; much, much bigger! The males carried big, backward spreading racks of antlers on their heads, with many sharp points. These animals had brown legs and a ruff of dark brown fur from their head down onto their necks. The rest of their bodies were a pale, greyish-tan. Their furry rumps had a yellowish tone. Little ones stretched their legs to keep at their mothers' sides.

These must be the elk he had heard about but what was their hurry? Their eyes rolled and their tongues lolled out. Up ahead of the rushing herd a massive bull stood on a jutting rock. He was calling out some kind of a warning to the herd in an odd, whistling, bugling voice – uruh, uruh, uruh. Suddenly Golden Eye saw the reason for their panic. Rushing up along the near side of the herd sprinted his nemesis, the Killer Cat! His golden coat stood out beside the herd as he ran with incredible speed. His muscles bunched and smoothed as he leapt along, swerving and swiveling, intent on one large female. Finally, with one mighty leap, the cat grabbed the elk around her shoulders, brought her down and, with one powerful bite, crushed her throat in his mighty jaws. The elk twitched, then lay still. The rest of the herd fled toward the trees, urged on by the lead male.

The big cat was about to begin his meal when his head suddenly snapped around. A current of wind had carried the scent of Golden Eye to his nose. Fresh kill or not, the Killer Cat spun around and rushed toward Golden Eye. Instinct took over and Golden Eye pivoted and ran with all the power in his legs into the crowd of elk, matching their pace and hiding in the depth of the herd. He turned his head to see if the cat was still behind him and what he saw amazed him! The huge bull, the leader of the herd, charged in front of the cat. He planted his hooves, lowered his head and, with one massive sweep of his antlers lifted and flung the mountain lion far off to the left! The stunned cat landed in a heap, snarling with shock, fear and anger.

He had, however, been given a stern lesson and therefore conceded that he was definitely not a match for the massive bull elk. He got up, shook off the dirt and loped off to wait for the herd to leave so he could enjoy his meal.

Golden Eye had stopped where he was too, as the herd moved away. When he was positive that the cat was gone, the big bull elk whuffed and turned toward his herd. Boy and elk looked at each other steadily. Golden Eye thought about how brave and strong the elk was and how grateful he was for its help. The elk stretched his nose toward Golden Eye, touching his chest. Golden Eye reached out his hand and stroked the soft fur of the elk's muzzle. It was a magical moment. Then the elk passed by and rejoined his family. Golden Eye made for the river's edge again, his mind in a whirl from all that had just happened.

Just before sunset Golden Eye came to the head of the long lake that he had been told about and there, just as they had said, were two canoes secured on the bank, resting under the leafy foliage of some alder trees. Golden Eye bathed, ate some huckleberries and drank some cold, clear lake water while he sat and thought for a few minutes. Not too far behind was the Killer Cat. True, he had a fat kill to fill his stomach but what of his other appetite - the appetite for overpowering Golden Eye?

"I think I will sleep out on the water tonight,"

Golden Eye said out loud to himself. "I'll paddle way out onto the lake where that wretched cat can't reach me and just curl up on my wolf-skin and sleep in the bottom of this canoe."

So he did, drifting off to sleep thinking about what tomorrow might bring, wondering how long this lake really was and how far it was to the mysterious caves he had heard about. Tree frogs sang a lullaby and an owl hooted in the boughs of a hemlock tree but Golden Eye didn't hear them. He'd been rocked to sleep in his watery bed.

Chapter Eight

Cat Chase, Wolf Rescue

Golden Eye awoke the next morning to a chorus of birdsong: first the lonely cry of a loon across the mist-shrouded lake, then robins, jays and sparrows and finally, the raucous croak of the raven. Golden Eye sat up and stretched, smacked his thirsty lips and slipped over the edge of the canoe for an invigorating morning swim. Wide awake now, he rubbed himself dry with the wolf skin and paddled away through the lifting mist; westward, away from the rising sun.

"This lake is a lot longer than it looked last night," he murmured to himself as the hours passed. His hands were well calloused so that he didn't develop blisters from all the paddling. He reached into one of his pouches and brought out a chunk of dried deer meat to chew on, giving power to his muscles and easing the morning growl in his stomach. Occasionally he dipped his hand into the lake for a refreshing drink.

The lake itself led westward and the shores to the north and south were distant but visible, hilly and covered right down to the shoreline with dense evergreens.

Finally, the end of the lake came into sight. Golden Eye scanned the shoreline and detected the place where another canoe was cached. He headed for that spot, climbed out onto shore and secured the canoe he had used. He took a while to walk along the shore and determine the path to follow. There were numerous animal paths leading down to the water: those of small creatures like rabbits and marmots, those of larger animals such as deer, bear and wolf, and finally, a well-trodden, clear path that could only have been made by centuries of human travel.

Golden Eye took time to eat some huckleberries and fill a bladder with water, then set off along the trail. The land rose steadily as he made his way through the natural pass in the range of mountains that ran down the centre of Protector Island. As he was passing a flowery meadow that covered an old rockslide, Golden Eye heard a sharp whistle. Up out of the ground, here and there across the meadow, furry heads popped up.

"Marmots!" whispered Golden Eye. "Aren't you little fellows just like big, fat squirrels?"

The glossy, dark brown creatures with their white bellies popped out of their burrows and scurried about, whistling to each other, wondering who this was passing through their territory. Golden Eye stopped and sat down on a rock. He plucked some small yellow flowers and held them out and shortly, after much scurrying about and bobbing up and down, one young marmot crept slowly and carefully nearer to Golden Eye, stretched out his head and took a nibble of the flowers.

Golden Eye was delighted that this chubby little creature trusted him. He kept very still and soon several other marmots crept close too and took their share of the tasty flowers. Golden Eye very slowly picked more flowers and some small berries growing close by. He held them out on his palm, next to his leg and before long, Golden Eye had a lap full of the happy creatures, mostly young ones he judged. The older members of the clan hung back by the entrances of their burrows, nervously watching their children. Golden Eye was entranced with the fat, furry creatures and tentatively stroked the fur of one that sat very still.

All of a sudden, one of the largest marmots, posted on a ridge above the meadow, gave out a loud, shrill whistle. In a mad dash, every marmot in the colony rushed to a burrow and disappeared from sight.

"What on earth…?" Golden Eye murmured, his senses on high alert.

Out of the underbrush beside the meadow charged the Killer Cat, his eyes blazing, muscles bulging, the black patches beside his mouth identifying him as Golden Eye's nemesis. The cat was leaping across the meadow in huge bounds. Golden Eye jumped up and sped along the trail. He had been running all his life along the trails of the hills and valleys of the Island of Salty Springs and up Crouching Mountain. He was a very fast runner and could run for hours at a swift pace, but apparently not as fast as the Killer Cat! The cat was gaining on Golden Eye, slowly but surely. He scanned the surrounding territory. Where could he hide, he wondered, or how could he elude the furry beast? There was no deep water nearby, the cat could climb any tree and climb it faster than he could and hills rose on either side. What could he do?

Golden Eye heard pebbles flung from beneath its paws as the cat approached. He rounded a turn in the path and saw a flat table of land where trees grew farther apart. Golden Eye veered into the woods, hoping to find a tree he could easily climb, hoping he could get to the thin top part where the cat couldn't reach him. Then, without a sound, a pack of wolves stepped out, one from behind every tree, to form a very large pack. One after another they padded forward, surrounding Golden Eye and forming a dense wall between Golden Eye and the Killer Cat.

The cat came to a screeching halt, throwing up a spray of pebbles, moss and dead leaves. A blood-curdling snarl ushered from the cat's fang-filled mouth, answered by a chorus of low growls, growing

louder and louder, from the wolves. Slowly, the pack
of at least twenty wolves advanced upon the Killer Cat.
The cat held his ground, hissing and swatting at the

lead wolf, all his claws extended. The lead wolf charged at the mountain lion who leapt up and came down upon the shoulders of the wolf. The wolf rolled on top of the cat and pulled himself upright. Killer Cat twisted and leapt to his feet. His head swiveled around, taking in the advancing wolf pack, and judging himself outnumbered, he charged away across the path and up a steep incline. Several wolves gave chase, snarling and howling, but were unable to complete the chase up the steep, rocky hill as rocks showered down on them from the paws of the nimble cat.

Golden Eye stood panting among the trees, watching the spectacle. Then, as the cat escaped, he sank down and rested with his back against a tree trunk. The wolf pack turned back into the tree line and gathered around Golden Eye. Most of them lay down, panting, their tongues lolling out, but the pack leader, an extra large, all black wolf, sat down on his haunches, facing Golden Eye, his nose mere inches from Golden Eye's face.

Golden Eye stared into the big wolf's eyes. He let his spirit take over and connect with that of the wolf. It felt as if his body just evaporated. He became a part of the spirit world, unconnected to things that could be touched. The sensation was very strange, like floating on top of still water with eyes closed, not seeing, feeling, smelling or touching anything; very strange indeed.

Golden Eye also sensed the spirits of all the wolves and of all the humans who had the wolf as their protecting spirit down through all time, endlessly. The period of this connection passed, leaving wolf and boy satisfied, full of understanding and with much gratitude on Golden Eye's part. This was the second really major encounter he had had with Wolf Spirit since he acquired their protection at his vision quest. He felt his spirit expand with each encounter.

The old wolf turned his head, sweeping his gaze over the pack and then silently, the pack melted back into the forest. Golden Eye wondered if they had really been of spirit or flesh. He watched them go then trekked away, up an incline to the top of a hill. Looking West he saw the head of an immensely long inlet and began trotting down toward it. He plunged forward down the trail but hadn't gone twenty paces when he was suddenly and frighteningly bowled over by a typhoon of golden fur, fangs and claws.

The cat was back!

Chapter Nine

Cave Shaman

Golden Eye and the Killer Cat tumbled down the inclined path, head over heels and sideways. Golden Eye instinctively held himself as close to the cat's body as he could, keeping himself safe from its claws while shoving its jaw upward with his right arm, preventing the killing bite to his neck.

"What am I going to do when we land?" he wondered.

His eyes spied a hole in the ground, big enough only for a mouse, so he let his spirit join with that of his grandfather the shaman, and poof, Golden Eye became a mouse and leapt down that tiny hole. The cat was again left wondering where his prey had disappeared to and he howled out his anger in a great, harsh scream. Back and forth he paced and dug furiously at the little hole where the scent was strongest; but to no avail. Eventually, as the lowering sun's rays glanced off his gleaming eyes, he slunk off into the bushes to clean himself and to nurse his hatred, hoping for his final deadly victory.

The mouse-that-was-Golden-Eye scampered down a tube-like tunnel. On and on in the darkness he scurried, not knowing where the tunnel led but preferring this mystery to the certainty of the furry death behind him! Finally he saw light ahead and as it got brighter he dropped with a plop onto a pile of small rocks. He was in a cave.

Golden Eye returned to his own shape and sat looking around. The cave was quite small. It looked like a giant hand had taken one scoop out of the hillside, so smooth were the limestone walls of this clamshell-shaped cave. He dusted himself off and stood up carefully. Pain shot through his body. He stepped out into the sunshine and checked himself over. Yes, there were a number of painful lumps, the beginnings of some major bruises on his head, shoulders, back, hips and legs. Of more concern were the claw slashes on his forearms, some of them bleeding quite freely.

"You need to wash those now," he heard a thin, reedy voice say from behind him.

Golden Eye whirled around nervously. There, on a large rock at the mouth of the little cave, sat the oldest human being Golden Eye had ever laid eyes upon. The old man had a bent back and supported himself with a wooden staff that was carved with the image of the legendary two-headed snake. His hair was sparse and silver and floated about the old man's bony shoulders. His face was so wrinkled it looked like sun-dried mud or the shell of a walnut, or most of all like a crumpled fish net. The old man's eyes were cloudy with age and his nose curved sharply, almost touching his toothless mouth. His body was bony and sinewy, muscles stretched scantily across his skeleton, with not a spare ounce of flesh on him.

A cape of marmot skins, loosely stitched together, hung from his right shoulder and wrapped around his waist and a collection of small deerskin pouches hung about his neck. His feet were encased in some kind of fur-lined leather, no doubt to protect him from the rocky terrain. The bones of his fingers, hands and wrists stood out sharply. Golden Eye sensed an air of wisdom and peace about him.

Rocks. All around them was nothing but rocks. They were in a gorge, possibly the bed of a former river, and surrounded by caves of all shapes and sizes. All about him Golden Eye could see caves; caves just big enough for a fox with barely an opening, caves tall and shallow with tree roots extending into them, caves even big enough for a family. "These must be the Upana caves," he thought, "and this the old hermit they told me about."

"Come on with me," said the ancient toothless one.

Golden Eye followed the old man down a boulder-strewn path and around a bend to where a small stream splashed down a slope. Golden Eye washed his skin, wincing at the sting of the deep cuts and the irritation of the skin scraped raw from his tumble down the hill with the cougar. Then the old one beckoned to Golden Eye to follow him. Golden Eye looked up in the direction the old man led and saw the edge of a cave mouth. He climbed up the few boulders to its entrance and as he moved into it his jaw dropped in amazement.

The cave was immense! Its opening was fifty paces wide and as tall as four men and roughly triangular in shape, but inside the entrance it opened up into an enormous room, bigger than the biggest longhouse Golden Eye had ever seen. The cave stretched back into the hillside so far that light could no longer penetrate its depth. Here and there sparkling white stalactites hung from the ceiling and shining white stalagmites rose to meet them. There were platforms on the left near the front, on the right a little higher and farther back plus another massive one just to the right of the middle of the cave, thirty paces in.

Golden Eye could see that the old man had made his home on this platform. There was a fire pit upon it and a few pieces of firewood plus bulging bladders, possibly of water and oils, and a little pile of animal furs – enough to make a soft bed for the bony old one.

Golden Eye followed the old man up the craggy steps to a rock near the mouth of his cave, where he motioned to Golden Eye to be seated. Then the old one proceeded to bruise and soften some leaves from a nearby stinging nettle plant and apply them to the cuts, stopping the bleeding. After that he created a salve of deer grease and more dried herbs which he spread onto

the bad scrapes.

"Is that stinging nettle you're using?" asked Golden Eye warily. "Doesn't it sting you to pick it?"

"You have to grasp the leaves so that those hairs are pressed in toward the stem, then it can't sting you. Look how fast it stopped the bleeding there. I make a tea from the roots or a hot poultice of bruised leaves for my achy bones in the wintertime too, or even strike the sore parts with the branches," said the old man.

"What are you putting on my scrapes?" asked Golden Eye. "My grandmother is a medicine woman. She would like to know what you use."

"Oh, that's what I call the healing herb, or knitbone. Helps to heal sores up quickly. Drink a tea of the whole plant to fix broken bones – that's why I call it knitbone. I'll give you some yarrow to take along with you. It will help too. There, how does that feel now?"

"Much better. Thank you very much. My name is Golden Eye, of the Salish people, protected by the Wolf Spirits. How may I address you?"

"I don't have a name anymore. I've been away from people for so long now that I no longer need a name. Sometimes the whaling people come near here and they holler out, 'Cave Uncle, are you there?' Sometimes I answer, sometimes I don't. Depends if I want any company that day. Of course, if they say that they have sickness or injury, I answer. The Great Spirit would be angered if I didn't help those in need of my medicine."

"My grandmother, Robin Song of the Salish people, shares her healing powers with everyone too, even wounded enemies. She says we are all of one flesh, all children of the same spirits, so we must all care for each other. I wish everyone felt like that."

"Sounds like a good woman, your grandmother," said the old one. "I see why you are called Golden Eye. Blessed by the Wolf Spirits, are you? How do you come to be here, young Salish boy?"

"I certainly am blessed by the Wolf Spirits," replied Golden Eye. Then he told the old one of his protection by Old One Eye during his childhood, his rescue by the orca Black Fin, the sea-wolf, and just that day by the wolf pack. He told him also of the lady in the water too, another of the Wolf Spirit protectors.

"You have done your vision quest then. Are you on another meaningful journey now?"

"I have a dream, Cave Uncle. I wish to meet and know the people of all the different nations; as many as I can anyway. I started near my Salish home and I hope to spend some time soon with the Nootka, the great whaling people of the western coast of Protector Island. I'm getting near them, aren't I?"

"Yes, you are very near them. I will send my thoughts into the mind of the shaman of the nearest village. Tomorrow he will send someone up the big inlet to meet you. You should say their name properly though. It is Nuu-chah-nulth."

Golden Eye struggled to pronounce the Wakashan word. However, having a mind eager to learn new things and a feeling of brotherhood with all people made understanding come easily to Golden Eye.

"May I ask how it is that you dwell alone up here in the caves?" Golden Eye enquired.

"You may ask young one. I am trying to understand all things and there is too much human noise in the villages of the people. My mind needs the quiet of this place to be able to think long thoughts. Do you know what I mean? Time and quiet enough to think something and then follow that thought, asking many questions in my mind, answering them and coming to a conclusion for the time being. I say for the time being because even though I have come to a logical conclusion at that time, future thinking and future experiences might add to the information supply and cause me to adjust my conclusion.

Also, it is so peaceful here, with the sound of the wind and the water and the creatures living out their lives around me, more or less quietly. Here I can be connected to the spirit world much more easily, all by myself. Have you ever felt this way, young traveler?"

"Why yes, Cave Uncle. I have often made a long run with only my wolf friend nearby to be able to sit and talk to the Great Spirit or to figure out what I really feel about things and whether I should be going along a certain path in my life."

"Good. You are a child of the spirits then, blessed by them. I can see that just by your special eye, like that of a wolf. So, wolf spirits protect you and guide you. Still, you must always rely on yourself as much as possible. Have your dream, don't be talked out of it by those who have given up on theirs, and follow that dream. Do not fear the unknown, listen to your instincts and watch for omens. The spirit world wants you to succeed. Yes, dream, but live in the here and now, enjoying each moment whether it is difficult or delightful. And while you are considering all these things, how about getting us some fire wood and spearing that fish that is coming down the stream over there in the woods. All this talking has made me hungry and your young muscles could spare mine for once."

"Gladly, Cave Uncle," cried Golden Eye.

Golden Eye chuckled and jumped up, wincing momentarily from the pain of his bumps and cuts. He followed the sound which led him to the nearby stream. He found a sharpened, forked stick propped up on a rock, picked it up and, lo and behold, just as the old man had said, a nice fat trout came splashing down the stream.

"Please give yourself to us for our dinner, friend

fish," said Golden Eye as he plunged the spear into the sparkling water. He pulled back the spear and on its end was a fat, glistening, wriggling fish. Golden Eye's mouth watered thinking how it would taste all crackling hot from the fire. He hurried back to the cave with his treasure, enjoying every moment.

As man and boy licked their fingers after the tasty meal, Golden Eye asked a question that had been on his mind.

"Will you tell me a little about these whale hunters I am going to visit, Cave Uncle?"

"Tell you about the people, eh? Well, as I said, their nation is Nuu-chah-nulth. That means Mountains-In-A-Row, because when you approach the area from seaward, that's what you see - mountains in a row. People can only build summer camps near the shore and on islands. Most of the permanent villages are well inland because of the winter storms. The one you go to is called Yuquot, The-Place-that-is-Hit-by-Winds-from-All-Directions, and the village is that of the Mowachaht, the People of the Deer.

The Western Ocean that stretches beyond the horizon so far that only the sun and moon have seen what is beyond it, sends waves crashing upon the beaches. Those waves are so big they could swallow a whole village and carry it away. It's a wondrous sight to see. Those big waves make a thunder of their own and the spray from them splashes high into the air and far onto the shore. You'll see. The trees near the shore are all bent and twisted by the mighty winds that blow along with those waves, and huge trees that have been ripped up farther away are flung up onto the beach. Lots of seaweed and rocks too. Very interesting to walk along there after a storm, it is. Find lots of different things. Are you staying through the winter?"

"No, I'm afraid not. I just wanted to meet those great whaling people. Then I'm going to join my friend in the village of the Kwakwaka'wakw people and be back home by winter time. Can you tell me more about the Nuu-chah-nulth people?"

"Hmm. Well, for the most part they are very strong, very proud. They have to be very strong to be able to hunt the whales. Have you ever seen one? They are as big as a longhouse! Maybe they'll see one and be ready for a hunt and maybe they'll take you along. You'll have to do the preparation rituals though.

Let's see now. Well, the people can live with the families of either their father or their mother. Makes it a lot easier. If you want to live in a village down the coast and your mother came from there, you just go on down and her people will take you in. Have to do your share of the work of course. But you wouldn't go if your father was Great Chief and had named you as his successor. You'd stay home then and learn how to serve the people. Your father would get the first of everything gathered, hunted or caught, because the spirits have named his ancestors the owners of everything in their territory. But, after he got the first bit, then he would allow the others to take all they needed.

Heh, heh, heh. It's funny to see them go after a wife for one of them from another village. Thirty of forty of the husband's family get very busy, gathering gifts for her family, getting themselves dressed up in their best. Then they all paddle down to her village and camp on the beach, singing and offering gifts to the chief and to her family until finally they are invited in. Then they can discuss the whole matter and, if the woman likes him and thinks she will be happy in his village, and if the gifts are accepted, then fine, off she goes to be his wife.

What's funny is, suppose they're all ready to go and the weather turns bad? They have to call the trip off, put everything away and wait, maybe until the next season and do it all over! Heh, heh heh.

They have lots of potlatches too, when they have to let everyone know about changes. Maybe a new chief, birth of a chief's son, giving away of rights to stories, songs, crests and things like that for a marriage. Or sometimes to honour a dead chief; maybe putting up a memorial pole for him too, things like that. And rituals. Oh, you might be in time for Tlu-Kwa-Na, the Wolf Ritual, too. Seems like you'd be a natural for that."

"What's the Wolf Ritual?"

"Never mind. You'll see when you get there. Go to sleep now. Someone will be here early to get you. Better slip up there and get your things. The cat's gone to bed now."

Golden Eye jumped, startled, remembering his wolfskin and his traveling pouches. How had the old one known about them and how did he know the cat was in bed?

"I know because you have the marks of having carried those things and I heard the cat go away. Nothing wrong with my hearing, boy. It's gotten better and better as my eyesight gets worse. It's some compensation anyway. Now go."

Golden Eye, amazed once again, scurried up the hillside, retrieved his belongings, which the cat had attempted to bury. He was soon snuggled in for the night by the lowering fire. He went to sleep watching the firelight flickering off the stalactites and poking little holes in the darkness of the cave.

Chapter Ten

On to Whaling Country!

"Hello!"

Golden Eye jumped up from his sleeping place. His head full of sleep, he didn't realize right away where he was or what had wakened him. He rubbed his face and took a deep breath to steady his rapidly-beating heart. Oh yes, he was in the big cave. Had he heard a voice?

"Hello, is anyone there?"

"Hello," Golden Eye called back. "We're in here."

Golden Eye scrambled down from the sleeping platform, noticing that the old man was still sound asleep.

"Klahoweya, tillicum - hello friend," Golden Eye said to the man who waited outside the cave. The man had broad, powerful shoulders and straight, raven-black hair that moved in the breeze. He wore only a woven cloth about his waist and stood barefoot, his well-muscled legs attesting to many hours - no, many years - of running. His face was sombre and unsmiling; a face that did not invite instant friendship, but a face reflecting strength and determination.

"I am Golden Eye of the Salish people on the Island of Salty Springs. Have you come to take me to the Mowachaht village?" he said, trying to correctly pronounce the name.

"Yes, I am that one," said the stranger. My name is He-Who-Harpoons-Best. Where is Cave Uncle? I have brought food for him for the winter: dried salmon, deer and bear meat and dried berry cakes."

"He is still sleeping. Please, come into the cave and we can share a morning meal."

"Only if he wakes up right away. We have a long voyage ahead of us and must get going if we want to get there before dark."

Golden Eye led the way into the cave and stood over the sleeping old man. The old one didn't awaken. Golden Eye deliberately made as much noise as possible while gathering up his possessions and building up the fire but still the old one snored on.

"Well, I think he is still enjoying his dreams so we'd better go," said Golden Eye.

"I'll leave his winter food and the medicine plants he asked for near his sleeping furs. He'll know that I've been here and that we left together. Come on.

The days are shorter now so we need to get moving. I heard a mountain lion snarling so we have to be on the lookout for it too."

"Yes, we really do," replied Golden Eye. "I have stories to tell you about that big cat, that's for sure. Now, where are those herbs that Cave Uncle gave me to take along for my wounds? Yes, the scratches are from that cat. See? All right I'm ready, let's go. Goodbye Cave Uncle, here's a branch of huckleberries to go with your morning meal. Thank you for all your help," he whispered to the withered old form under his furs.

With his wolf-skin around his shoulder against the morning chill, Golden Eye set off behind He-Who-Harpoons-Best. They moved briskly, climbing up out of the valley of caves, then heading down the last hillside toward the long ocean inlet that sparkled below them. The morning wind swished through the evergreen branches and dried leaves of the alder trees crackled under their feet as man and boy trotted along.

A woodpecker tapped at the trunk of a dead tree, seeking bugs for his breakfast. A blue jay swooped from tree to tree, chiding the travelers with his strident jaying; or perhaps he was notifying all the woodland creatures that people were coming. A rustling in the underbrush caused Golden Eye's head to snap to the side, fearing a visit from the Killer Cat, but it was nothing but a grouse, scuttling away from the passing humans.

The big harpoonist ignored everything around him and forged ahead at a trot. Golden Eye kept up with him easily, having been a long distance runner all of his young life. Golden Eye's mind wandered back to his many long runs criss-crossing the Island of Salty Springs. So many of those runs had been with his old wolf-protector at his side or nearby within the treeline.

Golden Eye reached one hand up to stroke the fur of his old friend and guardian, mentally thanking him for his companionship and protection ever since his childhood. Sadness mixed with happy memories inside Golden Eye's mind and heart. Then he began wondering how his other running companion, Tan Buck, was making out on his journey to visit the Kwakwaka'wakw people.

"We're on separate adventures for the first time, aren't we, my friend?" Golden Eye thought as a picture of his best friend's laughing face came up in his mind. Memories of their childhood explorations and the dangers they had lived and helped each other through flooded Golden Eye's memory as he jogged along the sun-dappled trail behind the silent man.

Thus preoccupied, Golden Eye bumped hard into the back of He-Who-Harpoons-Best, not realizing that the man had come to an abrupt halt.

"What...?" spoke Golden Eye.

A big hand clapped over his mouth before he

could say another word. Golden Eye peered around the man and saw, directly ahead, two small black bears. They were obviously less than a year old; no doubt born during their mother's hibernation last winter. One cub was sitting on his behind and the other was standing on his hind legs but both of them were slurping up huckleberries from a bush that overhung the trail.

"Their mother must be very near," whispered He-Who-Harpoons-Best. "Let's get off the trail and hope she takes them away...."

He didn't get to finish his sentence. Beside them, from behind another huckleberry bush, rose up a very big, very black, very fierce-looking she-bear. The two humans were between her and her cubs. Although they meant no harm to her or her babies, she was bound by instinct to attack anything and anyone who might pose a threat to her offspring. With an angry "waaaaah", the big bear charged out from behind the berry bush, straight at He-Who-Harpoons-Best.

The big whale hunter ducked and curled into a tight ball. Golden Eye did the same, right beside him. The mother bear slid to a halt in the small gravel of the path. She sniffed and sniffed the two humans, paying great attention to the wolf pelt covering Golden Eye with its head lying over top of his own. The two travelers didn't move, hardly daring to breathe.

Through slitted eyes, Golden Eye glimpsed the

huge claws of the mother bear as she paced, pigeon-toed, around them, occasionally pawing at them, sniffing and sniffing. He could see the two cubs too. They had scrambled up into a tree when their mother's actions had let them know that danger was near.

Still the travelers did not move and so, after a few more minutes, perceiving no real threat to her cubs, the sow shambled off. With a whuff she called her young ones out of the tree and the trio took off into the forest, ferns waving behind them.

"Whew, that was close," muttered Golden Eye.

"All in a day's journey," grumbled He-Who-Harpoons-Best, frustrated at being delayed on his trip. "Sometimes you can just stare into the bears eyes and walk away backward. Sometimes you have to make a big noise and wave a weapon or a stick and a bear will go away. Just don't ever run away. They run faster and you've become their prey then," he said coolly.

"The man has no feelings," thought Golden Eye. "At least no fear anyway."

Still, Golden Eye was extremely happy to have such a brave one as his companion on this trip. Golden Eye brushed himself off and reached into one of his pouches, pulling out some dried deer meat. He passed a strip to He-Who-Harpoons-Best and the man looked at the offering, nodded his head in thanks and took some. He then led Golden Eye to a small freshwater spring nearby where they took a cool, refreshing drink. They were on their way again.

At the head of the big inlet a two-man canoe awaited them, its stern straight and its prow jutting forward. They jumped in and pushed off, He-Who-Harpoons-Best in the bow. Each took up a paddle in silent communion, settling into a brisk rhythm as they headed down the immense tree and mountain bordered inlet.

Chapter Eleven

Place-That-is-Hit-by-Winds-From-All-Directions

Where the ocean entered the inlet, many miles from the start of their water journey, Golden Eye looked up. At the top of a high bluff stood a lone person, waving to the canoeists. He-Who-Harpoons-Best waved back and the hilltop greeter turned and ran off. Golden Eye could see that they had reached the shores of the great Western Ocean. There were some islands yes, but beyond them the ocean stretched far, far away. To the horizon there was nothing but water; endless, endless water.

Golden Eye asked He-Who-Harpoons-Best to pull into shore for a minute, then he ran up the rocky bluff and looked around. He could hardly believe what he saw. There were mountains behind him, craggy headlands with wind-bent bushes and arbutus trees all around him, lush tree-covered islands, long, long beaches stretching away on either side and that unbelievably green ocean stretching westward as far as the horizon.

And truly, like the name of the village, Yuquot, the wind did seem to blow from all directions. Golden Eye's fine black hair swirled around his head and face and his eyes sparkled with wonder. He ran back down to the canoe, then he and his companion paddled around the high bluff and pulled into a big hidden harbour.

Above its shores, above the highest of winter high tide lines, rose a very big village. Many longhouses stretched along the sheltered shore. They were horizontally planked with slightly back-sloped roofs, just like at home, but many more of them. Out in front of the homes were huge fish-drying frames. Long-nosed canoes rested on the banks below the longhouses, some small ones for local foraging, some big enough for travelling groups, but also some very sturdy-looking ones - big enough for ten men. These, Golden Eye decided, must be the craft in which these brave people set out to hunt the giant whales.

Many people ran down to the beach and some right into the water. They spread along the sides of the little canoe and, in a move that surprised but pleased Golden Eye, they lifted the canoe right out of the water, travelers still inside, and carried it up onto the shore! Laughing and talking all at once, they gathered around Golden Eye, touching him and patting him on the shoulders - a smiling, friendly welcome indeed! One man, a shaman from the look of him, sprinkled eagle down on Golden Eye's head. Then the crowd led him up to the house where the chief awaited, beckoning to Golden Eye to come inside his longhouse.

Golden Eye looked around for his traveling companion. He-Who-Harpoons-Best was back on the beach, stowing the paddles, ignored by the crowd and probably just as happy to be so ignored. Then he wandered up to join the people in the main longhouse.

The chief, whose name Golden Eye was told was Grizzly Slayer since the time he had won a battle with such a bear, indicated that Golden Eye should sit near him. Then he asked if the women had any food ready for the guest and his protector. The women and girls responded by ushering in long platters of steamed prawns and crabs plus oysters on their half-shells. Big bags of tea were shared around, to be drunk from the carved wooden cups brought forth from the storage boxes of the families that shared this home. Steamed seaweed went down well with the shellfish and soon everyone was satisfied.

"Thank you for this wonderful welcome," Golden Eye said to the chief, then spread his arms to include everyone who had helped bring him ashore or provided the meal. "I bring greetings to all of you from the Coast Salish, the People of the Salmon. For many years I have wished to meet you all, the Mighty Whale Hunters of the Western Ocean. It is my wish to be with you for a while, to become your friend and to learn your ways and your stories and perhaps to share some of my own."

"You are most welcome here, Golden Eye, Blessed-One-of-the-Spirits, Protected-One-of-the-Wolves. Enjoy your visit, please feel welcome in every longhouse in our village and in all our ceremonies. You have come at a good time. The humpback and the grey whales will be traveling south soon and perhaps you will see them. They are quite a sight! We may even be ready to go out and take one of them when they arrive.

Also, it is nearly time for the Wolf Ceremony. Surely no one would be more welcome into that than you. We have heard of your spirit blessings and the powers you have been given. We heartily welcome you, Golden Eye of the Salish People. May the Great Spirit lend blessings to your family and your village so that you will find them all well upon your return. Here is a whale bone necklace that I wish you to take home to your father, the wise chief Grey Fox."

"I want you to stay with my family," piped up a boy of about Golden Eye's age. "My name is Black Tail, like the deer. We have lots of room because I'm an only child and we have no relatives visiting just now."

"Hai-ch-ka, thank you," said Golden Eye with

his elbows bent upward and his hands open, palm out. as was the way with the Salish people.

"Come on." said Black Tail, "If you're finished eating, I'll show you where we sleep right now, then we can go see the seals. I can hear them out there on that rocky shelf. Can you? Let's go."

Golden Eye thanked his hosts and the servers and then left the big longhouse with his new friend. A whole group of young boys and girls followed them out, determined to be part of any adventure happening.

Chapter Twelve

Of Seals and Storms

On their way across the beach the young people examined the tide pools.

"Look here," called the girl named Pigeon Feather. "Here's a little octopus."

"There's another one over here, and three colours of starfish too," shouted little Owl Face, his eyes as round as his namesake.

"What is that floating in the water out there?" asked Golden Eye, squinting into the sun.

"That's a sea otter breaking clams on his belly."

"What? How can he do that?"

"Look harder. See? He brought up a flat rock and a small rock from the sea bed with one paw and a clam with the other. He laid the flat rock on his belly and now he's pounding the clam open with the little rock."

"Well, isn't he clever?" mused Golden Eye.

A chorus of "orks" drew their attention. The whole group quietly crept around a bluff to witness a colony of seals that had hauled themselves out of the ocean and were sunning themselves on the rocks.

"Shh," whispered Golden Eye. "I'm going to see if any of them want to go swimming with me."

The Nuu-chah-nulth children stared at Golden Eye with startled looks.

"Don't be silly. They might bite you or just ignore you or you'll scare them all away," chided Ptarmigan Wing, a boy of about Golden Eye's age.

"I got the idea from another boy's name. Stay here, I'm going to try," Golden Eye whispered back.

He slipped off his garment and slid noiselessly into the shining green ocean. He swam underwater until he was a short distance offshore from the seals, then he surfaced. He stayed with his head and shoulders out of the water for a few moments, until he could tell that some of the seals had seen him. The calls of the seals became even louder and they stretched their necks to the left and to the right, showing concern at this intruder.

Golden Eye took a breath and dove under the water, his feet making a small splash. He swam twenty breast strokes further away from the seals then surfaced again. One of the smaller seals began bobbing his head and very soon dove into the water himself. Within a few heartbeats, Golden Eye had a swimming companion, then two, then five. He dove and swam underwater, then surfaced and swam along the top for a while. Then back he went underwater again, leading the young seals nearer to his human friends.

Those friends stood open-mouthed as they watched Golden Eye swim with the seals.

"I guess he is as special as we've heard," said Black Tail, his young host.

After a while, Golden Eye swam to shore. The young people watched, astonished, as one of the smallest seals actually took Golden Eye's foot in his mouth, gently, trying to convince him to stay and swim with them.

"Sorry, little fellow, but I'm tired now and have to get back on shore. I'm afraid I'm not native to the water as much as your family. Black Tail, give me a hand up will you?"

Golden Eye pressed his feet against the steep rocky shore and Black Tail reached down, grasped Golden Eye's hand and hauled back, lifting Golden Eye onto the shore. The younger children crowded around Golden Eye, flooding him with questions about how it felt to swim with the seals, how did he understand them, wasn't he afraid and so on. The older children stood back and smiled, some chuckled and patted him on the shoulder as he freed himself from the little ones. Pigeon Feather offered him her blanket so he could dry off.

"We should get back to the longhouses. It looks like a storm coming in," said Pigeon Feather. "It's not safe for the little ones out here during a storm."

Golden Eye thought that was a strange thing to say. However, as the day passed, the wind became much stronger, howling through the openings in the longhouses. Some of the men went up onto the roofs and placed large rocks on the roof planks to make sure they didn't blow away.

Several hours before sunset time the older Nuu-chah-nulth boys invited Golden Eye to go out and watch the storm with them and he readily agreed. They all wrapped themselves in thick blankets and set forth. From the moment he stepped out of the longhouse, Golden Eye knew that this was unlike any storm he had ever witnessed. The strength of the wind sucked his breath out of him and nearly forced him back in through the doorway. The other boys formed a close pack and linked arms with each other, including Golden Eye in the middle. Bent forward, they forced their way up the back of a bluff between the longhouses and the ocean. Nearing the top, the wind was so strong that they had to get down on the ground and crawl. Their destination was a cluster of trees and they forced their way forward until they got within the midst of the wind-twisted trunks. Then they had something to hold on to while they watched the storm.

Golden Eye was astounded at the sight and sound of the storm. As far out as he could see on the ocean, huge waves were building and cresting. They were a fierce dark green in colour and carried foamy white crests on their tops. All along the miles and miles of curved white beaches those huge, mighty waves thundered and smashed onto the shore. One after another they pounded onto the beach with a noise like a gigantic fist smashing down. Where the boys huddled at the top of the high bluff, the spray from the waves that flung themselves against the rocky wall drenched the lads with salty water. The earth actually shuddered beneath their feet!

Golden Eye could understand now why the little ones had been taken to safety. He was feeling a thrill that he had never experienced before. The awesome power of nature that he was witnessing, the overwhelming strength of the wind, the pounding and smashing of the waves as they crashed onto shore then sucked back into their mother ocean were too much for his senses. Never before had he felt so small, so helpless in the face of such raw natural power. This ocean, that cove where he had swum so peacefully with the seals as small wavelets lapped the shore, had become a raging tyrant. Nearly alive with fury, it was like a great beast or some supernatural giant.

On and on the storm raged, with the wind whipping from all directions and each wave seeming to be larger than the last as the day waned and the sky darkened. The tops of the trees of the forest were being bent by the ferocious blasts of wind while those near the shore, being short and already twisted from earlier storms, were being whipped about and stripped of their leaves. Small bushes were simply ripped out and blown away at great speed. Incredibly, some seagulls were riding out the storm on the ocean, but far enough out that they were not thrown by the gigantic waves. Golden Eye wondered about all the other birds. Where were they hiding? Surely their nests would be blown away too. And what of all the sea life near the shore?

"Come on," yelled Ptarmigan Wing through chattering teeth. "Let's go home and get dry and warm."

The rest of the boys needed no more persuasion. They all backed carefully down the lee of the bluff, hanging on tightly to their blankets and each other.

They burst into the longhouse with a blast of wind behind them, causing those inside to exclaim loudly.

"Hurry!"

"Get the door covered!"

"Don't spray water on everything!"

"Get over by the fire and dry off"

"Here's some tea."

"Did everyone get back safely?" the comments rang out.

Golden Eye was silent because of the spectacle he had just witnessed. As he shivered and rubbed himself dry and gulped down cup after cup of hot tea, he thought what a great story this experience would make for his little brother Fat Goose, for his best friend Tan Buck and all the rest of his family back home on the Island of Salty Springs. A wave of homesickness passed over Golden Eye but just then, one of the Nuu-chah-nulth mothers gave him another dry, warm blanket and rubbed his chilled arms and back. The lonely feeling passed and he looked into the faces of all his new friends.

"That was something, wasn't it?" asked Ptarmigan Wing. "But by tomorrow, there'll be nothing to show for the storm but a thick line of seaweed and some new logs tossed up at the tideline."

"Hard to believe," replied the amazed visitor. He'd have to see that for himself!

Chapter Thirteen

Snake Woman

Golden Eye awoke the next morning to a strange sound, silence. For half the night he had woken often and could still hear the sound of the wind raging about and whistling through the cracks of the longhouse plus the thundering waves crashing upon the shore. He lay still and let his mind register the difference, adjusting his ears to the lack of noise, at least the lack of loud noise. There was the sound of people softly snoring all around him, which made him smile. From outside the longhouse, Golden Eye could hear the soft swish of a mild breeze among the branches of the cedar, fir and balsam trees.

He also heard the twitterings of the forest birds: the chickadees and wrens, the red-breasted nuthatches and band-tailed pigeons, the ruffed and blue grouse from the lower levels plus the tap-tap-tap of a wood-pecker higher up and his noisy neighbour the stellar jay. From shoreward he heard the calls of the eagles, the osprey and the kingfishers, on their morning fishing forays. An owl hooted far off and Golden Eye felt himself drifting back to sleep.

It wasn't long, though, until the families in the longhouse began to stir and then rise to begin their day. Golden Eye and the older children of the village gathered near the doorway and one by one stepped out. They breathed in fresh morning air that was scented with evergreens and the pungent, salty smell of the ocean and shore.

Some yawned and stretched, others scurried off into the woods to relieve their bladders. Golden Eye and a few of the older boys loped down to the shore.

"Look at all this stuff the storm blew in!" remarked Running Pheasant. "Look at that huge tree way up there." He pointed to a full-sized spruce tree, festooned with seaweed and tossed like a twig at least a hundred steps up from the water's edge.

"And look at all the crabs and starfish, and even clams," cried Golden Eye in amazement. "There's a bunch of sea cucumbers too. There must be a ton of seaweed along the tideline too, and, am I wrong? Isn't the tideline about twenty paces higher than it was yesterday?"

"You're right," replied Deer Foot. "So, that was your first west coast storm. Too bad you can't stay until it's really winter. Then you'd see even bigger storms!"

"Hard to believe a storm could be bigger than that," said Golden Eye in tones of wonder.

"Even at this time of year, we have to really watch out for signs of a storm. If the men are out whaling and get too far away, just imagine what one of those storms could do to them and their canoes," said Ptarmigan Wing.

"Will there be any whaling soon, while I'm here?" asked Golden Eye.

"It depends. We keep spotters up on the highest point of that ridge there. The whale hunters have been preparing for a hunt and the canoes for whaling are kept supplied and ready. They can be ready to push off very quickly when they get the word that a big grey or a humpback is spouting offshore. But if storm clouds are building out there, they have to let that whale and his family pass and hope for better weather the next time."

"What do they have to do to prepare?" asked Golden Eye.

"Oh, now you're asking about family secrets," replied Ptarmigan Wing in a low voice. "Every family of men has their own particular beliefs and rituals to get ready. One group I know of bathes three times a day, and each night they all meet in a secret place away from the village. There they might do a sweat lodge, drinking special teas and eating only certain foods.

They do other things too. Every group is different, but the whole idea is to make themselves tough and strong enough to take on a whale. Have you any idea how big one of those whales is?"

"Well, I've seen some pretty big killer whales, as big as ten men put together," said Golden Eye.

"Hah, that's nothing. A great grey whale is bigger than three hundred men! Just his tail is bigger than our traveling canoes and one slap with it can send a whaling canoe and all its crew to the bottom of the ocean, and humpbacks are even bigger!"

"Is that so? How do they expect to kill something that big?"

"It's all a matter of planning, having the right equipment, really strong, really brave men, expert harpooners and luck too. It depends if the spirits are pleased with the men's preparations and the whale's spirit has been convinced to end the contest by feeding us with his great body. Then if the weather holds, maybe the whalers will come home and maybe they will bring a whale home too."

"Incredible," whispered Golden Eye. "Do you think I could be with a family group while they get ready?"

"It depends. Have you bathed regularly on your way here?" asked Ptarmigan Wing.

"Oh yes. I've bathed in every stream, river and lake that I came to, so that the spirits would strengthen me and teach me."

"Well then, I'll ask my father and we'll see if you will be allowed. I'll let you know later. Come on, let's get some breakfast. I'm starved."

"Great idea. My stomach is growling too, but let's take a dip in the ocean first."

It was hard to believe that the great Western Ocean was calmly lapping at the shore after the way it had so furiously slammed itself upon the shore the day before. But the boys tossed off their garments and charged into the surf. The water was bitingly cold, refreshing and salty. The boys swam out a good distance from the shore, their muscular arms reaching ahead. Then they turned and rode the easy waves into shore.

They stood up, laughing and whooping about the stinging cold, and rubbed themselves to bring the circulation back to the skin. The boys grabbed their garments and dashed back to the longhouse for hot tea and a breakfast of hot octopus chunks dipped in oil. It was just the thing to stoke up hungry boys for a day of adventuring.

"How would you like to come along and help me gather some cedar bark, young Golden Eye?" asked a woman of the village. "I am Winter Wren. I have heard that you are strong with the spirits. I too am so blessed. Will you share some time with me, and help me?"

"Of course," replied Golden Eye. He gazed into the eyes of the woman. She had probably seen forty summers. Her face was unlined, her skin glowed in the firelight. Her long black hair hung in a thick braid nearly down to her waist. Her hands were very strong-looking, muscular, callused and reddened - probably from her work with cedar bark. Her eyes had the deep look that Golden Eye had seen in those of shamans and wise women, but with plenty of laugh wrinkles at the corners too. Golden Eye rose and said his thanks for the meal, promising to join his new friends later for some fun and adventure.

Winter Wren led the way out of the longhouse, picking up several baskets on her way. Golden Eye noticed out of the corner of his eye that some of the adults were leaning toward one another and whispering as they watched the two depart.

"Here, we'll take my little woman's canoe. We have to go north along the shore to a group of cedars that I have observed. I have to go farther each year to get the inner bark that I need. Can't use the ones right near home all the time - they need time to recover from the stripping."

"Your canoe is just about the same size as my own, back home," exclaimed Golden Eye. "My Uncle Raven Claw made it for me and it's just the right size for myself and my friend Tan Buck to go exploring. He has it right now, on his way to visit the

Kwakwaka'wakw people up north, on the other side of Protector Island."

"Oh, I know where the Kwakwaka'wakw people live," said Winter Wren. "We trade with them every year. We visit our relatives there and go to potlatches there sometimes. They are the biggest potlatchers of all. Here we are, we'll pull in here. Wait while I wave this soul-catcher around a bit. You never know when some unfriendly spirit is waiting in a new place - waiting to capture some unsuspecting soul. There, we should be all right now.

See those fine old cedars? I'll get plenty of stuff for weaving from them. Help me pull the canoe into this little stream and tie it to those branches, will you please?"

"Of course; and here, let me carry those baskets for you."

Winter Wren chuckled. "I don't usually have so much help," she said. "It's usually just me and another woman or girl, but who am I to complain about some help? Come on. I think we'll start with this tree. Hello, mother cedar tree. I ask that you give me some of your inner bark. I respect your life and will take only what I need and will not harm you unnecessarily.

Now then, Golden Eye, make a cut down near the bottom with that hatchet - that's right. Now make one up here. We have to remove the outer bark in between the two cuts - it's much too coarse and tough to use for weaving but we can take it home anyway, for the fire. Good, thanks. Now I will make a slice with my knife at the bottom, like this. Now I grab the fibres of the inner bark, like this and PULL, all the way up to the top of the cut. See what a nice long strip of inner bark that makes?"

"That's a beauty all right," agreed Golden Eye. "I've never seen finer. There sure are some huge cedars over here on Protector Island. I came through a grove of them on the way here that were so big that it took me several minutes to just walk around one! How old would you think those trees must be?"

"Hundreds of summers, those ones. Maybe some from the time of the first things on earth, when the Great Spirit looked down and began to make the perfect home for us, his people."

"Well, the cedar tree certainly was one of his greatest gifts, wasn't it? Food, shelter, clothing, canoes, firewood, carving material, medicine - what more could we ask for from one kind of tree?" Golden Eye said, counting things off on his fingers.

"That's right. Plus all the other kinds of trees we need and all the fish and berries we can eat. Luckily he gave us our brains and spirits too and the common sense to use all these gifts to share, to trade or to store up for the winter. Yes, we are lucky, lucky people, truly blessed by the Great Spirit. That's why we show our appreciation by taking only what we need, not wasting any, and not leaving a mess. See, I'm telling you this so you'll pick up all those pieces of bark. Go on, you're younger than me!"

Winter Wren laughed again at her teasing while Golden Eye jumped into action, cleaning up the area under the tree.

"How will you make this tough scratchy stuff into something nice enough to weave with?" Golden Eye asked.

"Soak it for three days in salt water, then pound it with a good rock and work it with my hands until it's lovely and soft. I have to cover my nose and mouth while I'm doing it though because lots of little particles fly off and my, are they irritating. We women have to cough a lot and go and wash our hair and face a lot to get rid of it."

"My mother weaves white dog hair in with hers," offered Golden Eye. "Do you have white dogs here too?"

"No. No white dogs, but we trade with the people from the Great Land for mountain goat hair and sometimes we get a little dog hair from your relatives over on the other side of Protector Island. Wait, what was that sound?"

"What sound?" asked Golden Eye.

"I hear a funny sound, like a hum or a whir. Don't you hear it?"

"No, I.....,wait...., yes I hear something!"

"I have to go and see what it is," exclaimed Winter Wren strongly. A strange, far-off look was in her eyes.

"But what if it's a swarm of bees or something awful?" cried Golden Eye.

"Don't speak anymore. My spirit is being called. Follow, but not too closely."

Golden Eye waited until Winter Wren had moved ten paces off into the forest then followed slowly, matching her pace, making no sound. Golden Eye had spent time with shamans and spirit women and he knew that a call like this mustn't be ignored and he must not interfere. Therefore he kept his mind quiet, his breathing soft and his footfalls gentle. He followed until he saw Winter Wren stop within a grove of alder trees. He watched her stand very still, obviously listening to a spirit message. Slowly she raised her head and looked above herself at the leaf-bare branches. Right above her head was a large bump or knot on one low branch.

Golden Eye took a few steps closer and gasped silently. The bump on the branch was moving - wriggling actually. Was it alive? Snakes! It was a ball of snakes! An incredible thing happened then. Winter Wren, in a trance, raised her hands, let slip her garment then lowered her hands and her head. Then slowly, slowly, the knot of snakes began untwisting and in a long stream slid down each other and all the way down

Winter Wren's body. For a little while Golden Eye couldn't even see Winter Wren, so many of the green wrigglers were passing over her. He wondered for a moment if he should go to help her but quickly realized that this was a powerful spiritual time for her and he decided to stay still. In a few minutes, every one of the snakes had slid down to the earth and they slipped away silently, into the leaf litter on the ground. After a moment Winter Wren raised her head and her shoulders, obviously taking a deep breath.

Then she did an amazing thing. She took one of those snakes and held it high by its tail, and she swallowed it, head first! Golden Eye stood like stone. After a moment, Winter Wren reached into her throat and pulled the snake out, tail first. It had turned from green to grey! She let the snake go, picked up and put on her garment, then turned and walked, somewhat unsteadily, back toward Golden Eye. He was amazed to see that her hair was now streaked in large patches with grey. Her facial features were frozen and she walked past Golden Eye, as if still in a trance, straight toward the canoe.

Golden Eye rushed to gather all the baskets, cedar and tools and stow them in the canoe. Winter Wren was already sitting in the canoe. Golden Eye untied it, jumped on board and picked up the paddle. He turned to check on Winter Wren. She reached out her right hand and touched the wounds on his shoulder from the Killer Cat. Golden Eye felt a ripple of shock pass through him. As Winter Wren removed her hand, Golden Eye looked at his shoulder and couldn't believe his eyes. The wounds were healing as he watched!

"I am now Snake Woman, no longer Winter Wren," intoned the woman. "I give thanks to the spirits for my new blessing. I have become a healer. Please take us home now"

Golden Eye needed no more encouragement and he began paddling hard to get them back quickly to the Nuu-chah-nulth village. But, as he pulled away from shore, he heard a sound that made his blood run cold; the scream of his nemesis, the Killer Cat, echoing from the forest they had just left.

"So, you're still after me, are you?" Golden Eye thought as chills ran up and down his spine. He dug in even harder with his paddle.

No sooner had Snake Woman stepped ashore at Yuquot than she reached out to a passing man who was limping because of a badly sprained ankle. She stopped the man and slid her hands down his lower leg and wrapped them around his ankle. The man gasped and jumped in surprise. Snake Woman let go of his ankle and the man took several tentative steps around.

"No pain!" he cried. "No pain. Thank the Great Spirit. You have healed me! Who are you, woman? I do not recognize you."

"I am Snake Woman, who was this morning Winter Wren. The spirits have chosen to bless me with healing powers. Now excuse me while I seek out others who need my touch."

Golden Eye watched this display of healing open-mouthed. As Snake Woman moved off, Golden Eye and the healed man put a hand on each other's shoulders and shook their heads. What could they say? Golden Eye secured the canoe and took the baskets into the chief's lodge where other women took them and placed them in the healer's quarters.

Word of the healing spread like wildfire through

the village and soon a group of people was following Snake Woman. She moved through the village, stopping where she sensed pain or suffering, entering longhouses and laying her hands on one with stomach pain, knowing somehow what was causing the trouble and healing the sick one with her hands. Another had a troubled spirit due to the death of her child. Snake Woman clutched the woman's head and ran her hands down the woman's sides, then placed both her hands over the woman's heart.

"Let peace be within you, child," she said.

The grieving woman began to cry, letting her grief out. Other women of the village gathered around her and stroked her hair or hugged her and truly she was at peace.

On and on Snake Woman went, healing injuries of the body and spirit until at last, near sundown, she went to her quarters and sank into a sound sleep.

At the evening meal all the villagers gathered in the longhouse of the chief, sharing their food and rejoicing together. Golden Eye had to tell the events of the morning over and over until everyone knew and could believe what had happened. Great was the celebration of this new gift that the spirits had sent them. Warm food and drink, warm friendships, family and great joy filled the longhouse that night and Golden Eye felt blessed too. "What other surprises will this trip hold?" he wondered.

Chapter Fourteen

Snot Boy, Mink Tricks and Torture

"Golden Eye," called Frog Man. "I have decided to include you in my family group's preparations for whale hunting."

"Thank you. Thank you very much," Golden Eye called back while trotting over to Frog Man's longhouse.

"My son, Ptarmigan Wing, tells me that you are both strong and brave. Are you able to keep a secret as well?"

"Oh yes!" Golden Eye replied. "I understand that each family's preparations are very private and I will respect that."

"Have you been bathing every day, even several times a day?"

"Why yes, I have. Ever since I heard the stories about the first of my people who bathed in every kind of running water they passed in order to strengthen their spirits I have been doing the same thing. So, yes, I am very thoroughly bathed and I intend to keep on doing it. I never know when I will need the spirits to protect me!"

"Good then. Come and eat with us this evening and then we will all go together. You may tell the great chief that you will be doing this with us, but never, ever tell anyone where we go or what we do to prepare. Do you promise?"

"I do, I promise," said Golden Eye.

His heart was beating faster just thinking about it. After thanking Frog Man again, Golden Eye ran off to find Ptarmigan Wing and quietly whispered the good news to him. Ptarmigan Wing grinned and slapped Golden Eye on the back, showing his pleasure. They didn't speak about it any further because there were many young people about, there on the beach. Some of them were scattered along the ocean shore, still searching for interesting things that the storm might have tossed up. One group was gathering clams - some digging, some prying them open, some carrying baskets of them up to fill with fresh stream water. Golden Eye knew that they would soak for three days, then be dried and rubbed with oil so that they would be good for many days.

One of the small boys near Golden Eye and Ptarmigan Wing sneezed suddenly and the boys looked at him. Streams of mucous ran down from his nose.

Ptarmigan Wing couldn't help it. He laughed at the sight.

"That reminds me of a story my grandfather used to tell me, called Snot Boy."

"Snot Boy?" asked the incredulous Golden Eye.

"Yes, Snot Boy," chuckled Ptarmigan Wing, joined by all the nearby boys and girls.

"His name was Andaokot and his mother had lost her children to a supernatural being, long, long ago before everything was as it is now," began one girl.

"And she cried so much, all the time, because her children were gone, that one day while she was bent over, some snot ran out of her nose...," yelled Black Tail, doubling up with laughter, unable to continue.

"..and it turned into a tiny boy, who grew very fast," chimed in another girl.

"He vowed to make his mother stop crying and he worked to make himself extremely strong," added Ptarmigan Wing.

"Then he went and found that mean supernatural being, fought with him and defeated him. He brought the children back to their mother so she finally stopped crying and was happy," said Puffin Girl.

"Then he shot a line of arrows up into the sky and climbed up to the Sky World. There he was given instructions by the Great Spirit after which he returned to Earth and transformed all things into their present

state," concluded Ptarmigan Wing.

"And to think that he started out as just a clump of snot," shouted a young lad. "So be careful when you sneeze, little one, you might get yourself a new brother!"

Everyone laughed until their sides were sore.

"Look! See that little mink sneaking into the underbrush there?" whispered Puffin Girl. "Kwatyat, he is called. His ancestors were transformers, able to change themselves into anything. Our southern cousins, the Makah, believe that he arranged the whole landscape as it is - stealing daylight from its owner for us - even timing the tides so that the people could get the clams and mussels and things. He's supposed to be a real trickster."

"Yes," agreed Ptarmigan Wing. "There's a story about how he defeated a pack of wolves."

"Tell us the story," begged little Splashing Water.

"Well, it is said that after a great battle, Kwatyat killed the Wolf Chief. Then he had to run away really quickly because the rest of the wolves were after him. Just when the wolves were almost upon him, Kwatyat stuck his magic comb into the ground and a huge mountain sprang up between him and the wolves. On and on he ran but after a time he heard the pounding paws and the snarls of the wolf pack - even felt their hot breath blowing upon him. So what did Kwatyat do? He pulled out a small pouch of oil, poured it onto the ground behind him and the oil became a great lake across which he swam to safety and which the wolves could not cross. Then Kwatyat, the trickster mink, laughed and slipped into the woods, just like that sleek, shiny one we just saw."

"I like the one about when Mink beat the Thunderbirds," piped up another boy. "There was a place down the coast there, where the Thunderbirds liked to gather to play a hoop game. Well, Mink watched them and then asked if he could play too. The Thunderbirds said yes and Kwatyat the Mink joined the game. All along though he had been thinking about how to beat the Thunderbirds. He used his magic to make the hoops go crooked whenever the Thunderbirds played so that he would win the game.

After a while the Thunderbirds caught on to what he was doing and they stomped on him and sent him away. Well, Kwatyat the Mink decided to have revenge. He lured three of the giant birds from their mountaintop home by turning himself into a whale in a vessel, knowing they couldn't resist a meal of whale. There he caught them one by one and pulled them under the water and drowned them. You see that big rock down there? He turned his vessel into that."

"Great story!" said Golden Eye.

"All right everyone; lets finish getting clams and seaweed before the tide turns. I guess we have Kwatyat to thank for this nice low tide," grinned Ptarmigan Wing.

Later that day Golden Eye joined Ptarmigan Wing's family for the evening meal of clams in a hot broth with bits of delicious seaweed swirling about. This was followed by big steaks of halibut and camas root, the tasty potato-like vegetable that Golden Eye remembered collecting with his grandmother back home. Wooden bowls of huckleberries and bladders of salal tea were passed around to finish the meal. Golden Eye thanked the women and girls for preparing the meal and they smiled and nodded to show that he was welcome. Golden Eye noticed that the men known to be whalers had not eaten.

Late that night, Frog Man whispered to the men of his longhouse to rise and follow him. Silently they filed out, looked around and, seeing no one in the clearing, made their way to their big canoe on the shore of a lake near Yuquot. Just as silently they paddled away, making a place for Golden Eye and handing him a paddle so he could do his share.

Within a short time they beached the craft on the shore of a small island in the lake where they pulled the canoe up and covered it with fallen leaves to conceal it. Silently, every man slipped into the water of the lake and bathed themselves thoroughly. Still without speaking, they followed a path through the thick undegrowth, single file, holding back branches that might have whipped back to smack the faces of those following.

Darker and darker it became as night came on and the woods became even denser. Then suddenly they burst into a large clearing. At its end was a cluster of carved images of whales and men plus a few human skulls. An old chief lived there, tending the shrine and calling the whales near shore, Ptarmigan Wing told Golden Eye.

What followed caused Golden Eye's mouth to drop open in surprise but he overcame this and got right into the ritual. He knew how honoured he was to be included in their secret rites. Ptarmigan Wing had told him that every family had their own special ways of preparing for a whale hunt. This was his family's way.

By the light of the rising moon only, the men were facing each other and grasping each other's shoulders. With muscles bulging and neck veins standing out, each struggled to overpower the other. Ptarmigan Wing tapped Golden Eye on the shoulder, indicating that they should do this too. With a small thrill of excitement mixed with a bit of fear, Golden Eye brought his hands and arms up, outside those of Ptarmigan Wing and grasped the other boy's shoulders. Ptarmigan Wing did the same to Golden Eye and the contest was on. Planting their feet firmly on the ground, the boys bent toward one another, each struggling to try to force the other off balance.

Even in the chill night air, sweat began to form on their foreheads, their faces, then their bodies, making it even more difficult to maintain their grasp on each other. All of a sudden Ptarmigan Wing swung one foot forward and hooked his leg behind Golden Eye's knee. Down they went onto the ground with a thump. Then the struggle became one of legs - whose leg could gain the advantage over the other's. Twisting and

turning, rolling on the ground, the two boys wrestled with their legs, just as the older men were doing. There was no anger in the contests, they just seemed to be competing together to strengthen their muscles. All this Golden Eye sensed as the struggles went on in silence broken only by the occasional grunt.

Then, as if at a given signal, Ptarmigan Wing

held up his hands in front of Golden Eye's face, stopped leg wrestling and held out his hand to help Golden Eye stand. Following his friend, he joined the circle that the men had formed. The oldest one whom Golden Eye recognized as one of the shamans of the village, brought forth a large bladder and went round the circle, pouring a long stream of liquid into the mouth of each man.

"It must taste awful," Golden Eye thought as he saw these big strong warriors's facial muscles tense and their noses flare as they took their share. Indeed it did taste ghastly he realized as his mouth was filled to overflowing. He fought to keep himself from gagging.

"To purify the blood." the shaman whispered softly into Golden Eye's ear.

"All right, if you say so," thought Golden Eye, feeling the horrid liquid burn down his throat into his stomach. Around him he heard everyone else taking in gasps of air too, just as he did.

Then all the men took a step foward and the circle became smaller, more intimate. At a signal from the family chief, they all sat down and each one reached to the left with their right hand and the right with their left hand. Golden Eye did the same and felt the power of the group as they connected in this way. This surge of power seemed to remove all feeling of time and place, as if they all became part of one thing, one being. Time stood still for a while and then the moment passed.

The leaders of the ritual also shared family secrets of medicines for toothaches, ulcers, lung infections and other illnesses. They also led the men in songs to the Great Spirit out of respect and to ask guidance.

Then back they trudged, single file, to the shore of the lake where they all bathed again. Golden Eye thought they would be leaving then but no. By the light of the moon, across which a thread of cloud passed, the men each collected a branch from a pine tree.

"Oh, oh," thought Golden Eye. "What now?"

He soon found out. The men paired off again and took turns scrubbing each others' backs with the pine boughs. Golden Eye faced Ptarmigan Wing and indicated that his friend should do this to him first. He wanted to know how it felt, although he could imagine it, before he had to do it to his friend. He turned around.

Scrape! The first scrubbing caused Golden Eye to suck in air sharply. His eyes watered, sweat beads formed on his forehead, his hands clenched in reaction to the sharp, stinging pain of the pine needles against his back.

"I'm not doing it very hard," whispered Ptarmigan Wing.

"Thank the Great Spirit that you actually like me," Golden Eye whispered back. "I'd hate to think what it would feel like if you hated me! Why are we doing this again?"

"To make us tough and able to withstand lots of pain. When we go after a whale we have to be prepared to do our part no matter how much pain is involved."

"Oh, all right then. Ouch," Golden Eye whispered as the pine bough assaulted his already tender back once more. "I think it's your turn now. You have to get brave and tough too, don't you?"

"Yes. All right, here's the branch. Now don't be too kind. I've been doing this for a week now and I'm getting used to it."

"A week of this!" thought Golden Eye as he scrubbed his friend with the pine bough. "It hurts just thinking about it."

All around them the grown men were doing the same thing to each other. He saw that the men stood tall and accepted the painful ritual stoically, dripping blood, but not even flinching.

"They must have to endure a lot of pain when they're whaling if they have to put up with this just to get ready," he whispered to Ptarmigan Wing.

"Oh yes," replied his friend. "A whale could destroy one of the huge whaling canoes with one flap of his tail so just think what that could do to the men inside it! Also, we have to keep up with him when he is harpooned and swims away. Then we have to paddle all the way back to the village. Some people have broken arms or legs or head injuries or bad cuts. Some men may even have been drowned. You have to be tough enough to do your part and not complain through all that. And that's why we fast and pray to the whale spirits and to our protector spirits and do these things.

We have to be ready to put our lives on the line in order to bring home enough food for the whole village from one whale. Think of all that meat and all the oil from the blubber. Think of all the big bones that can be made into tools and needles and the huge stomach and bladders for storing oils."

"Be quiet over there!" hissed one of the older men.

As morning neared, the family chief pointed to the star cluster called The Elk that was shaped like a small water dipper. The ritual was over. They silently dressed, uncovered the canoes and paddled off for home as the shadow of the moon rippled over the water and a chorus of tiny frogs echoed from the trees.

Golden Eye reflected that he now understood why so many Nuu-chah-nulth men slept on their stomachs!

Chapter Fifteen

Whale!!!

For four days, the same group of men walked off at certain times, bathed in ten different streams and continued their nightly ritual at the lake. Other groups, he noticed, went off in other directions. Then, one morning Golden Eye was standing at the end of a long rocky outcrop that jutted out into the ocean. He was thinking about what a wondrous place this was with its beautiful beach curving away for miles to the north and to the south. He looked at the mountains all in a row behind him, the islands dotting the coast, the craggy bluffs of Yuquot and the ocean itself. It stretched as far as he could see and yet lapped gently and rhythmically up onto the beach. Golden Eye drank in all the sights with his eyes and breathed of the fresh, salty breeze while seagulls called their creaky song and funny-faced puffins whizzed by.

Suddenly he heard someone shout, "Cicilnii!"

Golden Eye turned toward the sound and saw, up on the highest point of land, one of the young men of the village. He was waving toward the village and he hollered again, "Cicilnii!"

"What's he saying? Golden Eye asked BlackTail.

"Grey whale! He's spotted a grey whale."

Golden Eye ran back to the village as fast as his legs could carry him. The whole population was in action. Some men were moving the big whaling canoes out into the water. Others were on board the canoes, checking that all the supplies were ready: harpoons, ropes, huge bladder floats, food and water. Some were pulling on their whaling clothes - thickly furred hide wraps belted with leather thongs and their pointed-domed, downward curved, rainproof hats.

Someone passed an elk hide to Golden Eye and he quickly arranged it over his left shoulder and evenly down his back and front. He secured it with a length of rope, into which he tucked his fine, obsidian-bladed knife.

Within minutes the whaling fleet of the Nuu-chah-nulth set out. Ten canoes - each twenty paces long, eight men to a canoe, paddling out in the direction of the whale. Great Chief Grizzly Slayer was at the head of one canoe and He-Who-Harpoons-Best at the head of another. On the way out, one man in each canoe had the job of blowing up the air bladders, which had been soaking in the stream to keep them pliable. Golden Eye, Ptarmigan Wing, and Black Tail followed in a smaller canoe as observers, although they carried extra water, air bags and harpoons as well.

"What kind was it?" yelled the great chief to the lookout boy as he took his place.

"Cicilnii! A grey whale," he yelled back .

"Hmm, too bad." grunted the chief.

"Why is it too bad?" Golden Eye asked Ptarmigan Wing who was paddling just in front of him.

"Well, for one thing, they're smaller than our favourite, the humpback. We only get five hundred bladders of oil from them, just half what a humpback gives. For another thing, they're much more ferocious than humpbacks. More people might be hurt or killed."

"Oh," said Golden Eye, wondering what he and they were in for today.

"This must be one of the ones that live around here all year. The travelling herds of greys usually don't pass here until the last moon of the year."

From the other canoes Golden Eye heard a spotter sing out. He had seen the whale spouting - blowing spray out his blowhole - ahead and to their left. Moving as one, the canoes angled off toward the ocean leviathan and before long they were near where it had been seen. The men maneuvered to approach the whale toward the sun so it wouldn't see their shadow but the whale had dived. The men stopped paddling and waited. They didn't have to wait long.

Suddenly it seemed as if the ocean itself was rising and two canoes flew into the air as the great grey whale surfaced underneath them. Men and canoes, paddles and supplies, were scattered over the surface of the ocean. The great chief took advantage of the extreme nearness of the whale and launched the first harpoon as he was arcing through the air. The head of the harpoon struck home beneath the fin of the huge creature. The chief jerked loose the long shaft, leaving the sharp harpoon head, attached to a float, embedded in the whale.

The great beast reacted to the sting of the harpoon and dove. The float, made of a sea lion bladder, followed the whale down into the water but a few minutes later the men saw it surface.

Golden Eye looked around and saw that the men who had been flung about like feathers had righted their canoes. They quickly gathered their floating gear and helped each other back on board. Some had blood streaming down their faces, arms or bodies but all had grabbed their paddles and were in hot pursuit of the whale. As they paddled they chanted a loud song, promising the whale great honour and happiness if he would swim toward shore. The whale ignored them.

The back of the cicilnii rolled into sight before them, headed away toward the horizon. A great spout of spray rose from its blowhole. Then its head disap-

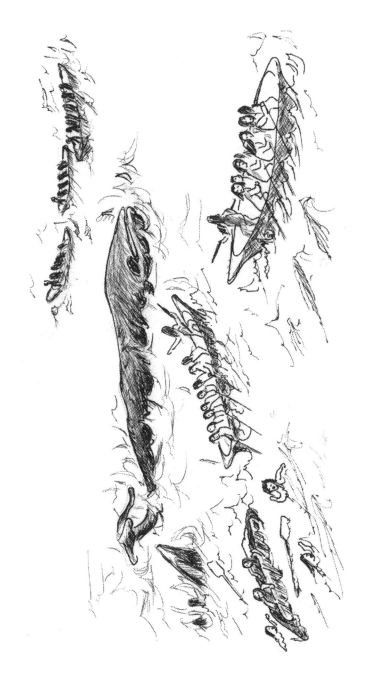

peared under the surface again as its massive back continued to roll up and away.

"Look out!" came a warning from one of the canoes. Too late. The great beast raised his enormous tail fluke and crashed it down on several of the canoes. Most of the men on board managed to jump clear as the canoes disappeared under the water. The huge splash had also created a big wave which caused Golden Eye's canoe to rise and tip and fall about on the foamy surface. The boys grabbed onto the edges of their canoe and held on tight until the water settled again. Within moments the whalers had righted their canoes and gotten back on board, hauling in their floating equipment once more.

Chief Grizzly Slayer knew where the whale would surface and made an overhand signal to the men to paddle fast and approach in a wide circle. As the whale rose within harpoon range the chief gave an underhand signal. Three men rose and Golden Eye saw that three more harpoons had found their marks in the hide of the whale with their big, air-filled bladders trailing behind. He-Who-Harpoons-Best had managed to score a very deep one, in front of the right side flipper.

"Die, Devilfish!" he screamed at the whale.

One of the big canoes that had been smashed by the whale's tail had some damage to a side and some of the seats but it was still whole and strong. One man's left arm was hanging down uselessly and he grimaced.

"Here, hold him," yelled one of his mates. Other men held the injured man still and the one who had yelled grabbed the hand of the useless arm and tugged straight out to the side.

"Ahhh!" screamed the injured man, then he sat down and grinned. "Thank you!" he exclaimed. His shoulder had been dislocated and had been popped back into place! Off they all went again in pursuit of the cicilnii.

Now the great beast decided to stop playing around with these annoying people. And, since the floats were keeping him from diving too well, he decided to just swim away, so he did. Full speed ahead, that big-as-a-longhouse leviathan surrounded by floats began swimming southward, followed by the canoes. The men and older boys paddled hard to try to keep up. At one point the whale slowed and He-Who-Harpoons-Best took the opportunity to go near and drive home the killing lance.

Day slowly turned to night. A squall blew up and the whale hunters, rain streaming down their faces and bodies, had to bail water from their canoes. They struggled to keep their canoes upright in the lashing wind and choppy waves that accompanied the storm.

Golden Eye and Ptarmigan Wing did their share of paddling and bailing too. Very few of the woven hats had survived the dunkings and most paddlers struggled to keep their eyes clear and their sore muscles working during the long hours that the whale led them southward.

As dawn of the second day broke, Golden Eye awoke. The squall had passed and the sun rose in a blaze of glorious colours, glinting off the green ocean swells. A few seagulls floated on the surface, rising and falling with the easy swells, but nowhere could Golden Eye see a trace of land. His heart leapt within his chest. Never before had he been out of sight of land; never had he been further than a few minutes from a shore. "Have we entered the Spirit world?" he wondered. "Will I ever see my family again?"

Golden Eye looked around at the other canoes as the sun climbed above the horizon. In all the ten canoes, men and boys were waking and stretching, nudging those still in slumber. "How could we have ever slept?" Golden Eye wondered. He had woken to find himself in a curled-up sitting position on the floor of the canoe, just in front of his seat. Others had done the same or were stretched, as best they could, across a seat. Some were along the canoe bottom, side-by-side, with feet under one seat and head under another or on someone else's feet.

All at once it seemed to occur to everyone at the same time that they, and the canoes, and the great grey whale, were immobile upon the ocean. The Great

Chief struggled up to his feet, climbed upon the front seat of his big canoe and stared at the whale ahead of them on the water. The great beast was indeed absolutely still. Blood no longer ran from his harpoon wounds. There were even some sea-birds perched upon his mighty back.

With just a gesture, Great Chief Grizzly Slayer indicated that they should paddle up beside the whale's head. Golden Eye watched as the sea hunters cautiously approached to within a few paddle lengths of the huge creature's eye. Even from there they could see that the whale was dead, his eye glazed over.

As one, all the hunters raised their hands and arms and began a chant. Golden Eye understood that they were praising and thanking the spirit of the whale. He had fought a great fight but in the end had given his body to the people and had set his spirit free.

As the last notes of the beautiful, haunting chant died away across the water, the whalers brought their canoes together near the great beast's head. One man took hold of a rope and dove under the whale's jaw, coming up the other side. Other men tied the great mouth shut so that it wouldn't take in water and slow them.

"Is anyone missing?" asked Grizzly Slayer, scanning the canoes.

"We're all here," replied He-Who-Harpoons-Best. "Strong Arm is badly hurt though; smashed by that beast's tail. Maybe we can get back in time for Snake Woman to help him. I don't know though. He's hardly breathing and there's bloody foam coming from his mouth."

Men from other canoes reported that this man or that had a broken limb or ribs or were dazed from head wounds, but most were still able to paddle. All the canoes were still seaworthy, though some bore signs of whale damage too.

"Well, let's head for home then. It may take days, towing this big fellow," said Grizzly Slayer, reaching out one hand and patting the hide of the whale.

The men got busy tying all the rest of their floats to the great grey whale's carcass so that he would continue to float and not sink as they towed him home.

"Where's home?" Golden Eye wondered, but the men seemed to know somehow. They watched the sun as it walked its east-to-west path and the canoes travelled northward. They watched for shore birds to the east and paddled closer to shore, avoiding any rocky outcrops where the whale might be grounded.

Golden Eye took time out to make a potion for Strong Arm out of some of the healing herbs he carried in one of the pouches hanging about his neck. There was no way to boil water of course but still he hoped it would help a little. Strong Arm took small sips, wincing in pain as he tried to swallow. He smiled his thanks to Golden Eye and then laid his head down again.

As night of the second day drew on, the men began to take turns paddling and sleeping, each for a few hours. That way they could keep moving toward home - albeit a little slower - but getting some rest too. Their food was nearly gone. They shared their dried fish and deer that had been stowed in waterproof boxes attached to the hulls. Water too was shared, the most valuable commodity. All about them was an ocean so vast that its measurement was unfathomable, and yet it was undrinkable, it was so salty. The canoes had been stocked with bladders of water certainly; but eighty men, all working hard at their paddles, all eating dried fish and meat, were in need of a lot of water, and theirs was nearly gone.

Late in the morning of the third day, they came near shore and heard a very welcome sound. Falling water! One canoe at a time, they landed on a gravelly beach where a stream met the ocean. Someone from each canoe grabbed up the water bladders and rushed to the little waterfall that tumbled down the cliff side above the beach. They took this marvelous opportunity to get out of the canoes and stretch their legs too.

What a great feeling that was after days in the canoe, sitting on hard seats, paddling day and night! Just to feel their muscles straightening and stretching was a great tonic for them all. They also took the time to make a softer, more comfortable resting place for

Strong Arm and to wash wounds and bind broken limbs. Then they somewhat reluctantly got back into the canoes and began towing the giant carcass toward home again. Many seabirds rested upon the whale now, smelling death and hoping for a meal.

At mid-day, they heard a hail and looked toward shore. Six canoes approached. They were filled with men from their neighbour village, the Hesquiaht people. They were warmly greeted and soon they had attached lines to the whale too. Progress was greatly speeded up then, with all those extra paddles and fresh, strong arms helping. As the sun neared the horizon, the mighty Nuu-chah-nulth whale hunters heard the shore lookout calling to announce their arrival home. As they got nearer they saw that all the villagers were standing atop the longhouses, waving and cheering. What a wonderful, welcome sound that was!

They let the tide help them bring the great beast to shore and everyone pitched in to haul it up onto the beach. The women and cousins of the chief came down with a measuring mat and cut up the carcass. The chief had his speaker direct them as to who got how much from which part of the whale. The Hesquiaht neighbours were of course given a share to take home but they stayed and took part in the feast that night to celebrate the bringing home of so much meat and oil.

In fact, so much oil was rendered down that they filled all their sea-lion, cod-fish and even dog salmon stomach containers. Oh, but it tasted wonderful as they dipped their roasted whale meat into it, and some salmon too.

Golden Eye ate heartily but he was certainly glad that the Oo-simch, the preparation rituals, and indeed the hunt itself, were over. He was tired bone and sinew. He noticed that the women of the whalers now began to comb their hair. Black Tail whispered to Golden Eye, when he mentioned it, that they feared to break a hair if they combed while the whalers were hunting, in case the harpoon line should break. Neither did they eat or drink during the nights the men were away for fear they might affect the size and fatness of the whale.

Golden Eye shook his head in wonder at all he had learned so far about the famous whalers of the wild west coast.

"What next?" he wondered. He would soon find out.

Chapter Sixteen

Tlu-Kwa-Na, The Rites of the Wolf

All the whale meat had been preserved and stowed away. All the precious oil hung up high. All the sinews and bones, the stomach, lungs and bladder had been cleaned, dried, oiled and put away. Hundreds of berry cakes had also been dried and stored plus tons of fish and shellfish. Food for the winter was assured and a time of rest came to the village. Golden Eye and He-Who-Harpoons-Best made a day's voyage to take a canoe full of food to the hermit shaman and see if he was well. They found him in good health and spirits and he welcomed the food plus the dried herbs, seaweed and new bearskin they had brought him.

Golden Eye kept a weather-eye out for the Killer Cat but the only sign of him was a dried pile of droppings on the trail - a distinct warning that he, the wildcat, had laid claim to the area. The trip back was uneventful and a glorious sunset greeted them as they paddled out of the long inlet and rounded the bluffs toward the village at Yuquot. A pallette of purple, pink, orange and yellow painted the sky and the thin clouds. The next few days passed pleasantly but then people began to act nervously. Someone thought they had seen a large wolf circling the village, just across the creek. The sightings became more frequent and the small children were kept very close to the longhouses. Then, one night, a wail began to go up from the various longhouses. Women were crying that their older children were missing. Children mourned for their brothers and sisters.

"The wolf has taken them," they cried.

Golden Eye looked all over for his friends Ptarmigan Wing and Black Fin but nowhere were they to be seen. Then that night a hand clamped over his mouth and he was silently lifted, firmly held, and carried out of the longhouse. Away into the forest he was carried. Finally, he was set down. By the sliver of a moon he could see all the boys of around his age and some girls too. They were all huddled in groups. There were men there too. Men with long-snouted wolf masks on their heads and shaggy blankets around their shoulders.

The wolf-men howled and danced in a circle while other men stood around the perimeter of the young folk. Golden Eye found Ptarmigan Wing and sidled up to him.

"What's happening?" he whispered.

"Pay close attention. We are the fortunate ones who will be initiated into the Wolf Society. Our parents have paid the elders of the Society to train us. We must learn the Wolf Dance and be able to perform it, plus the dances of other animals and birds. When this is over, we will be taken back to the village and if we do well, we will be invited into the Wolf Society. It is a great honour for us and even more so for you, the only outsider who has ever been invited. Someone must have sponsored you," his friend explained.

For the next few days, the young people practiced. Hour after hour they practiced. They were not allowed to see anyone of the village except the elders of the Wolf Society and the drummers and chanters that beat out and sang the songs of Tlu-kwa-na.

Golden Eye and the other initiates were given wolf-like robes to wear and wolf headdresses of their own. By watching the wolf-men, they learned to dance bent over and to twist their heads this way and that so that they actually began to seem like wolves. Those who learned quickest were also taught the dances of other creatures.

Golden Eye was thrilled to the core of his being to be included in the training. His thoughts traveled back to his old wolf-friend, One Eye, who had run with and protected Golden Eye all of his life. At night he stroked the pelt of his old friend as it covered him, protecting him from the late autumn chill.

"I feel your spirit near me still, old friend," he thought as he drifted into weary slumber.

Late, late each night, the young dancers were secretly hidden in the back end of the most distant out-building of the village. Before dawn they were taken back into the forest, far enough away so that they could not be heard and that no one from the village might stumble upon them.

Finally, one evening just after sunset at the dark of the moon, they were led back to the village. The covering of the big entrance to the Great Chief's long-house was swept aside. There the whole village was gathered and a huge fire burned at the centre of the Great Chief's longhouse. Drummers and chanters were lined up on the raised platforms along the edges of the longhouse. The first to enter was Wolf Man, leader of the Wolf Society, who had supervised the testing of the young dancers himself.

The fire crackled and popped, sending sparks flying high into the air and out through the smoke holes. Wolf Man lead the troupe of young people in a snaking path between the fire and the circle of villagers. The dancers bent and twisted as he did, lunging at the villagers who reeled back, pretending to be afraid of the fierce wolf pack that danced before them.

Around and around the pack of wolf dancers circled and spun, spreading their wolf robes with their

arms, pounding out the wolf dance. They searched about, but for what? Did they seek food for their young? Did they seek revenge for their brothers who had been taken? They snapped open and closed the mouths of the wolf headdresses they wore. Some of the smaller children in the audience hid behind their parents, unsure whether these apparitions were really a threat to them or not.

Golden Eye had been allowed to wear the hide and head of Old One Eye. It had been tightly secured to his back and his head but he had to keep his head well down to hide his face. What he saw most of all as he danced was the feet and legs of his fellow dancers and the laps of the villagers as he approached them. The pounding of the drums and the chant of the singers, combined with the excitement of the night and the oneness of the dancers, began to make Golden Eye feel like he had indeed <u>become</u> Old One Eye. He began to howl and the other dancers picked up the cry and howled too.

The drums and the chanting stopped. The whole longhouse was filled with wolf howls, echoing off the roof and wall beams. It seemed as if the whole village had become a wolf pack. The walls seemed to melt away and the forest to surround them. It was a truly magical moment. Then, as the young wolf dancers stopped their howl, an answering howl was heard from out among the giant cedars. Then came another from across the stream, and another from up on the hillside and so on until the world seemed consumed by the haunting, soul-searching sound. Did the wolves know that they now had many new human brothers?

As the wolf howl faded away, the villagers of Yuquot came back to themselves and back to the confines of the longhouse. The young dancers were accepted into the Wolf Society, then they were welcomed back by their families and congratulated and a great feast ensued.

Golden Eye rolled up Old One Eye's pelt and sat among the happy revellers, his eyes shining and his spirit knowing a new depth - a new and deeper connection with his protecting spirit, the wolf. Later, when all the food had been eaten or put away, when all the costumes had been carefully stowed away in their beautiful carved boxes, Golden Eye gazed with sleepy eyes into the embers of the big fire.

"My body lies here in this longhouse," he thought "but the real me is out there in the forest with you, my wolf brothers."

As his eyes closed in sleep, Golden Eye thought he heard the snuffle of a wolf outside the walls. He smiled and pulled his friend's pelt closer yet.

Chapter Seventeen

Cross-Island with Air Walker

"It's time for me to be getting on my way," Golden Eye announced. The days were growing shorter and colder. "I want to meet up with my friend Tan Buck at the village of the Kwakwaka'wakw nation and get home before winter sets in," he told his new friends.

"Well, you'll have company on the way," announced Ptarmigan Wing.

"Oh? Who else is going?" Golden Eye asked.

"That girl over there by the huckleberry bush. Her name is Air Walker. She's special too," Ptarmigan Wing chuckled. "She is from the main village of the Kwakwaka'wakw people. She has been visiting her aunt here, also of the Kwakwaka'wakw, who married one of my uncles. Air Walker is descended from a long line of shamans and spirit women. It shows when she gets really interested in something. She rises above the ground! She doesn't even realize it when it's happening. We've learned to just take her hand and bring her back down. She never actually floats away; just sort of drifts a little way above the ground. It's kind of funny actually," explained the boy, while trying hard not to laugh out loud. The facts just amused him so.

"So that's why she seems taller sometimes," exclaimed Golden Eye. "I wondered about that. I thought maybe she had an older sister who looked a lot like her."

"No, it was the same person. Come and meet her. Good Morning, Air Walker. This is Golden Eye of the Coast Salish people. I know you've seen him around here but he is about to leave on his way to your home village. Since you are heading there too, our elders have decided you should travel together."

"Hello, Air Walker," Golden Eye greeted the girl.

She seemed to be of about his own age, maybe twelve or thirteen summers old. She was a little taller than he, thinner and with shining black hair that rippled down to her waist. She had a pleasant face and a gentle, friendly smile.

"It is good to meet you, Golden Eye," replied Air Walker. "I have seen you around here, doing the Wolf Dance and helping with the whale hunt. I'll be happy to have your company travelling back to my home."

"I'll be happy to have some company too," said Golden Eye. "Could you be ready to leave soon? I'd like to get going tomorrow if possible."

"Oh, yes. I just need to tie up my blanket and say goodbye to my friends and relatives here and we can be on our way, today even, if you want. I'm anxious to see my mother and father and my little sister, so we can leave whenever you say."

"Good. Let's plan to leave at first light tomorrow then," said Golden Eye.

He and Ptarmigan Wing stayed near Air Walker for a little while, picking themselves handfuls of the last of the sweet red berries. Then Golden Eye began making the rounds of the groups of young people and adults that he had met and with whom he had shared exciting times. He wanted to thank so many of them and to say goodbye face to face, imprinting their faces and personalities into his memory. Who knew how long it might be before he would see any of them again? He promised himself that if the opportunity arose to travel here for trade or any other reason, he would be very glad to return to Yuquot, where the wind blows from all directions. He already had many new friends, fantastic memories and great stories to tell back at home. He smiled just thinking about coming back here sometime.

The next morning, bright and early, Golden Eye and Air Walker set off. They left in a small, two-person canoe much like Golden Eye's own. Up a long, north-stretching inlet behind the village they paddled, thankful that the tide was running in. Pairs of puffins with their fat black bodies and colourful, wide, hooked beaks whizzed past, hurrying to their favourite fishing places.

"You're a good paddler," he called over his shoulder to Air Walker.

"Thank you," she replied. "You do pretty well yourself for a boy your age."

Golden Eye had to smile about that. He wouldn't be underestimating Air Walker from now on or thinking she was any less capable just because she was a girl.

By mid-day they had reached the end of the long inlet and they hopped ashore and secured the canoe above the tideline.

"Well," said Golden Eye. "that was a different inlet from the one I arrived by. I'm hoping you know the right paths to take us to your home village."

"Don't worry," she said. "I've done this before. There are good paths overland to a pair of pod-shaped lakes. They empty into a good river that takes us to a really big lake, called Nimpkish. At the end of that there's a short river ride out to the northeastern corner of Protector Island. That's where my village lies. It's more protected than Yuquot, being on the inside of the big island but probably the weather is a little wilder than at your home village because we're so much farther north."

Golden Eye and Air Walker set off at a brisk pace; their feet swishing through the fallen leaves. Some of the deciduous trees were completely bare now but others still shone with autumn colours amidst the dark evergreens. Above them the occasional vee of geese honked, heading southward.

"Tell me something about your village," Golden Eye asked.

"Well, my village is called Xwalk and it is spread out along the coastline. There are many Kwakwaka'wakw villages, some on the islands and even up the inlets on the Great Land. There are actually thousands and thousands of people but at the main village only about five hundred. We probably wear the same kind of clothes as your Salish people and the Nuu-chah-nulth, aprons woven from the inner bark of the cedar, plus blankets with mountain goat or dog hair and even some feathers woven in. We trade a lot with the people on the Great Land as well as with the Island people. Did you know there's a branch of your Salish people over on the Great Land across from the Kwakwaka'wakw nation called the Bella Coola? Their language sounds very much like yours."

"Yes, I know that. Maybe Tan Buck and I will get to visit them. It all depends on how long this fine autumn weather holds out. I certainly want to meet your people too before I head home. Are things very different there from the Nuu-chah-nulth ways?"

"Oh, there are certainly some differences. We don't go whaling anywhere near as often as they do. Let's see, we eat a lot of salmon, cod, halibut and trout. We dry lots of berry cakes for winter and seaweed too, just like your families, I suppose. Ooh, and oolichan oil too, yumm. Our men catch some oolichan in an inlet on the Great Land but we trade for lots more with the Salish people who live by the Sto'lo River on the Great Land across from your home. As you know, the oolichan run up that river every spring by the millions.

One thing that's different is the number of potlatches we have. Some of my uncles are completely caught up in a sort of competition to see who holds the most and the biggest potlatches. You should see it! They have to build extra houses just to store up all the things they're going to give away: blankets for some potlatches, canoes for others, food, boxes and things for marriages; carvings, clothing, dentalia shells. It gets bigger and better every year and there's hardly a space of time in winter between them! Maybe you'll see when we get there."

"Why do they have so many potlatches?" asked Golden Eye.

"Well, sometimes to celebrate and let everyone know about a birth, a marriage or a girl's coming of age or if, for instance, a father transfers his rank to his son."

"Rank?" queried Golden Eye.

"Yes, you see there are four clans, named for the first four humans of our nation. They came to earth in the dress and mask of the Thunderbird, the Wolf, the Whale and the Sun. Now in every village, each person belongs to their father's clan. Then, too, each village is ranked in order of importance. My home village happens to have four tribes. The number one tribe is called the true Kwakiutl, then the Kweka or Murderers, the Walas Kwakiutl or Great Kwakiutl and last the Kumkutis or Rich Side.

Of course, there is order of importance within each of these too, from the chief on down but men can compete by putting on big potlatches to try to claim a higher rank from someone else. Then, if the challenged one can't put on an even bigger potlatch in return, the challenger might succeed and claim the higher rank."

"Sounds very tricky but I'll bet there are lots of great feasts to go along with them. My friend Tan Buck will love that!"

"Then too, there are the secret societies."

"Oh, like the Nuu-chah-nulth Wolf Society and our Spirit Dance Society?" asked Golden Eye.

"I guess so. Ours are named the Hamatsa or Cannibal Society, the Grizzly Bear Society, the Hamshamtses, another so-called Cannibal Society except they don't use whistles in their dances, the Crazy Man Society and the Warrior Society. Pretty scary names, right?"

"They really are!" exclaimed Golden Eye. "Am I in danger of being eaten?"

"No, no," Air Walker replied. "I think it makes the men and boys feel braver to have scary names."

"Well, I'm glad of that!" said Golden Eye.

"Also, boys can belong to the Sea Parrot Society until they are of thirteen summers, then the Mallards until they are of sixteen summers and finally to the Killer Whales. We girls have our own societies and initiation ceremonies too, with feasting, dances and gift giving.

You really must see the coppers though. There are seven famous coppers. They're shaped like a shield; flared at the top and ridged down the centre of the bottom half. Just one is worth all the goods given at a big potlatch."

"Very interesting!" exclaimed Golden Eye. "Where did they get those coppers? My father owns a little bit of copper but no one else in our village has any."

"There is some around here but most is from a place on the Great Land, far up northward among the Tsimshian people. It's a very secret place and my uncles' ancestors traded for them - as much as five thousand blankets for one! They are considered a symbol of great wealth, rich culture, spiritual power and even magic for one's health. They are brought out in a cradle with blankets at naming ceremonies and the new copper and the baby are named at the same time. They come out for marriage and dowry ceremonies too.

There's an elaborate ritual involved in purchasing a copper. The owner must be given blankets that are worth one-sixth the value of the copper. The owner then lends the blankets out to his family members. At trading time he must give back twice that many. An offer is made of the lowest price ever paid for the copper and the owner agrees but, his family members argue and keep raising the price until it is more than the last price paid.

Sometimes a chief may actually break his copper and give pieces to a rival. Then the rival must break a copper of even greater value so he won't be outdone. One chief I've heard of actually threw his copper into the ocean, proving that he was so rich he could do that. Another really rich chief threw his into the fire! I guess that made everyone know he was the richest. Once though, a chief's son died and the chief laid his copper over his son's grave and it was never sold again."

"Whew," Golden Eye whistled. "Sounds very, very important to own a copper. What are they named?"

"Oh, things like Qualoma, the Beaver Face, Maxtsolem or Other-Coppers-are-Ashamed-to-Look-at-It, Nenqumala or Bear Face; Quoyim, the Whale and Lopelila which means Making-the-House-Empty-of-Blankets."

Golden Eye had a good laugh about that.

"No wonder the house is empty of blankets if they're worth that much!"

"But, there's one that's called Causing Destitution. It must be cursed because everyone who has owned it has died a horrible death or become extremely poor. And yet, people go on buying it for more and more, thinking they will be able to break the curse, but they never do."

"That's amazing," replied Golden Eye. "I certainly hope none of your family own that thing."

"No, not any more," said Air Walker. "My family and all my uncles families just want to keep having bigger and better potlatches so they don't want to own something like that."

They both had a good laugh then.

Air Walker and Golden Eye had been walking for miles now along a path that was visible but somewhat overgrown. Sometimes, true to her name, Air Walker would get excited, talking about her village, and would rise off the ground, actually walking along through the air. Golden Eye would begin to notice that her head became higher and higher and he would gently take her hand and bring her back to earth. This was quite a mind-boggling thing to him but he tried not to make a fuss about it as it seemed quite a natural thing

to Air Walker.

"There are a lot of spiritual creatures in our culture too, such as U'melth, the Raven who brought us the sun and moon, fire, salmon and the tides. Also Tseiqami, that you know as Thunderbird, Lord-of-the-Winter-Dance, Komokwe, the Undersea Chief; Sisiutle, a three-headed sea serpent, Pugwis, a fish-faced sea creature with big front teeth, Dzunukwa..."

"I know that one!" cried Golden Eye. She's The-Old-Woman-of-the-Woods-Who-Eats-Children, right?"

"Yes," smiled Air Walker. "And there's my favourite, Bakwas, The-King-of-the-Ghosts. I've heard he is small and green with a skeleton face and a long curved nose. He lives in the forest where he tries to bring the living into the world of the dead."

They had veered off to the left of the main path and decided to take a short break. They chose a spot under a hazelnut tree and pounded open some fallen nuts between two rocks.

"Just like the sea otters," Golden Eye observed.

"Yes," agreed Air Walker. "I think they're so adorable with their sweet little whiskered faces and their sleek, shiny fur. And their babies are so cute. They ride around on their mothers' backs sometimes too. The squirrels haven't left us many nuts have they?"

"No. I guess they're storing up food for the winter too," said Golden Eye. "There's a few huckleberries left on this bush here."

As Golden Eye stood up to step over to the huckleberry bush, he was suddenly flattened to the ground. The Killer Cat was back!

Chapter Eighteen

Oh No, Not That Cat Again!

Golden Eye hit the ground with terrific force. He felt the weight of the big cat on top of himself and instinctively wrapped his arms around his neck. He had learned that mountain lions quickly kill their prey with one swift bite to the neck, severing the big veins and usually breaking the neck at the same time.

Something was strange though. Golden Eye expected to feel the great cat's claws gripping him, its muscles tightening, fangs biting into his flesh, and hot breath searing his face, but no! He felt none of those things; just the full weight of the beast on top of him.

Golden Eye lowered his head and arms, pulled his knees up and gave a mighty heave to his right while rolling to his left. He unsheathed his knife as he rolled.

"What's wrong here?" he thought. "Why isn't he trying to kill me this time?"

Golden Eye sat up, then stood up, pulled Air

Walker down to the ground from among the lower branches of the nut tree, and stared at the Killer Cat. It lay silent and still on its side, clearly unconscious. But why? Golden Eye looked around and realized that the momentum of its lunge onto his back had propelled the big cat's head into the trunk of a large old yew tree.

"Well, I always knew yew wood was as hard as stone. This proves it. That poor cat has probably killed himself instead of me," intoned Golden Eye, shaking his head in disbelief at his good luck and the cat's bad luck.

Air Walker swallowed hard and cleared her throat before she could speak.

"What do you mean, that POOR cat? That thing tried to kill you!"

"Oh, I know, he's been trying to kill me ever since I set foot on Protector Island but he's been foiled every time. He certainly is a beautiful creature though, isn't he?"

"Wellll, yesss," she had to admit. "Is it dead?"

"Let's see."

Golden Eye warily approached the big, beautiful cat that was lying so still across the path. Sunlight filtered through the branches of the trees and made a pattern on its fur.

"He's still alive," Golden Eye whispered. "His ribs are rising and falling slightly and I can feel air coming from his nose - really slowly though."

"What shall we do, kill it?" asked Air Walker in a small, quivering voice. "After all, it's been trying to kill you, and, it would make a wonderful fur robe."

"Oh no!" Golden Eye replied immediately. "We can't kill this beautiful creature! Let's try to help him. If he's just asleep for a while we can hurry away as he wakes up, but if he's hurt, maybe there's something we can do. Help me turn him over. He looks and feels fine on this side, no broken bones, no bleeding that I can see."

With some effort the two young people very carefully rolled the mountain lion over onto his left side.

"Oooh, there's some of the trouble," said Golden Eye. His right front leg is dislocated. See how it just hangs down loose like that? We might be able to fix that. I saw the whalers pop an arm back in place. Let's try. You hold his shoulder and upper body really still."

"Great Spirit, please help us in this effort, and PLEASE, keep the cat asleep while we do it," prayed Air Walker out loud.

Tentatively, Golden Eye lifted the cat's flopping leg, rested it on his shoulder, and felt for the joint into which the leg should pop. When he was sure of the place and the angle, he lifted the leg straight out from the shoulder joint, placed his left foot on the cat's chest and gave a mighty pull then let go!

"Did you hear that little clunk?" Golden Eye asked Air Walker in an excited whisper. "It went back in! See how much more naturally the leg lies now?"

"All right, the leg's fixed. Now, should we get going before he wakes up?" Air Walker asked fervently.

"Not yet," said Golden Eye. "We need to put something cold on his head where he bashed it. Oh my! Look at his eye."

Golden Eye had lifted the lid of the great beast's right eye. The white was all red.

"He's been hurt inside his head and it bled down into his eye. Now we have to stay and take care of him for sure. He's absolutely helpless until he wakes up."

"Oh, great," grumbled Air Walker. "Babysitting a mountain lion. One that could wake up and eat me any minute. Just what I wanted to do today," she said sarcastically.

"It might not be too long and then we can get back on our way. But just look at him. He's so beautiful and he was so proud and so strong. We can't just leave him to be killed by wolves or to have his eyes pecked out by birds. He's one of the Great Spirit's creatures, just like us. Let's make a cold pack from this thick moss and some water from that nice, cold spring over there. That's right, put it on his forehead where he banged it. Good. Now let's make a little fire and get comfortable. This might take a while."

"I wish Snake Woman was here," mumbled Air Walker. "Maybe she would be able to just lay her magic hands on him and fix him and we could get going. I'm sorry, Golden Eye, but when I saw that great big thing leap on you, I was scared out of my wits. You disappeared underneath him and I thought you would be killed for sure. Then I thought I'd be next! I'm sorry but I'm having a hard time feeling very sorry for that creature."

Golden Eye chuckled and patted Air Walker on the shoulder reassuringly. They got busy then and built a small fire. Then, because it looked very much like it would soon rain, they built a lean-to shelter out of branches and ferns.

"There, nice and cozy, right?" said Golden Eye, smiling.

"It will do for the night," conceded Air Walker. "I'll go snare us a rabbit or a grouse for evening meal before it rains. I need a little distance between myself and that Killer Cat for a little while anyway."

While she was gone, Golden Eye covered the big cat with his wolf pelt and made sleeping pads of soft cedar boughs. He made his pad right beside the cougar and lay down beside it, sharing his body warmth with it. Golden Eye sent his thoughts out to connect with those of his grandmother Robin Song, the healer of his village plus those of his grandfather, the shaman, Strong Oak.

He gathered their souls together and called to that of Snake Woman and the old hermit healer. Then he closed his eyes and wished that they might all together appeal to the spirits to help the big cat heal and be well. Golden Eye felt himself to be part of a warm, colourful circle. A circle of power, but a circle of humble supplication to the spirits so that they might lend their help to these humans and to this creature of the forests and mountains. He seemed to hear a drumbeat and a chanting, deep within his head.

After a while, the period of connected prayer ended. Golden Eye came back to the present time and place and looked around. Darkness was gathering and behind him, Air Walker was roasting a fat grouse over the fire. Beside him, the Killer Cat's side rose and fell in good, regular breathing. Golden Eye put his ear against the cat's side. He heard, not only a strong heartbeat, but a purr, an actual purr!

"Listen to this," he called softly to Air Walker.

She gave Golden Eye a look that said he was crazy, that she'd rather put her foot in the fire than get next to that feline killer, but she finally crept over to it. Golden Eye moved away and Air Walker tentatively laid her head on the cat's chest, since its eyes were closed, since its legs were still, and she heard it too.

"Well, that's probably a good sign," she reluctantly agreed. "All right, let's share this food and then get some sleep. We have a long way to go yet. Also, since it was your idea to stay here with this giant human-eater, you get to sleep between IT and ME, do you understand?"

Golden Eye chuckled but agreed. The two of them hungrily devoured the juicy, delicious feast of roast grouse. Then they washed up and got settled for the night, drifting off to sleep to the sound of the crackling fire, tree frogs chirping and a hunting owl hooting off in the forest.

Chapter Nineteen

Big, Furry Tagalong

The light and the sounds of morning woke Golden Eye. His body was warm under his half of Air Walker's blanket but the end of his nose was cold and there was a film of dew on his face and hair.

Golden Eye sat up and looked around. The fire had gone out. Air Walker was not in her sleeping place. "Probably gone off to empty her bladder," Golden Eye supposed. The big cat lay just as he had the night before, still breathing regularly, so Golden Eye got up quietly and made his own way into the bushes beyond the cougar.

Crack!

Golden Eye froze where he stood and slowly turned his head in the direction of the sound behind him. There stood Killer Cat, gazing intently at Golden Eye! Instantly, all of Golden Eye's senses were on alert, ready for whatever might happen next. The wisdom of his shaman grandfather steadied his mind.

Killer Cat took a tentative step toward Golden Eye, keeping eye contact with him all the while. As Golden Eye didn't move or make any noise, the big cat took a few more slow steps forward until he was just a few steps from Golden Eye. Then he stopped, and sat down.

"What now?" thought Golden Eye.

The boy slowly, very slowly, knelt down to face the cougar. Boy and cougar looked into each other's eyes. Then the big cat did a strange thing. He raised one paw and wagged it, making little pawing motions toward Golden Eye. After that, it stretched its head forward and rubbed the side of his face on Golden Eye's left arm. Golden Eye instinctively reached around the cat's neck with his left arm and laid his head on Killer Cat's own head. The big cat began to purr again!

Golden Eye could hardly believe what was happening. The warmth between them was like that he had experienced with Old One Eye, his wolf protector, but that relationship had begun when Golden Eye was a tiny lad and had grown through the years.

With tears in his eyes, Golden Eye looked at the cat's face again, checking its eye and its forehead, and feeling the shoulder that had been dislocated. The mountain lion seemed to be all right, except that its eyes were a little bit crossed now!

"Well," Golden Eye murmured, "you are acting

a bit weird for a mountain lion. Maybe your brain got a little bit scrambled from that bump on your head. Maybe it knocked all the nasty out of you or maybe I smell like your family to you now. Anyway, whatever it was, I'm sure glad we're friends now and you've stopped hunting me down. Come on, do you want to go back to the campsite with me? I have to get going toward the Kwakwaka'wakw village with my friend. What are you going to do, boy?" Golden Eye asked of the cougar.

The big cat simply stood up and followed Golden Eye, walking close to his side. Air Walker was rolling up her blanket as boy and cat moved into the campsite. She whirled and when she saw the cougar awake and at Golden Eye's side, her eyes became huge. She gasped and clutched her blanket to her chest and began to float.

"Wh-what's happening?" she whispered.

"It seems I have a new friend here. Look at his eyes - they're a little bit crossed. I think that bump on his head changed him somehow; or maybe he realized that we were helping him and are his friends. I don't know, but anyway, he's my friend now. Shall we get going toward your village?" he said, while hauling Air Walker down to earth.

"Is that creature coming too?" asked the incredulous Air Walker.

"I guess we'll have to see if he follows us. Lets go."

Golden Eye rolled up and tied his wolf skin with a leather thong and slung it over his shoulder and the three of them set off. Air Walker made certain that she was on the opposite side of Golden Eye. She still didn't trust that big cat. Suppose he came to his senses and went on the attack again?

Killer Cat, however, seemed quite content to trot along at Golden Eye's side. He did make one quick dash off into the underbrush and the other two heard the sound of a small creature's demise as Killer Cat found his morning meal. A short while later he rejoined them on the trail, licking his chops.

"Well, I'm glad at least that I don't have to feed you, big fellow. You seem to have remembered that much."

"As long as he doesn't remember why he wanted to kill you, that's all I hope," muttered Air Walker, rising slightly above the trail as her worried mind thought about that possibility.

Golden Eye took her hand and brought her back to earth again and the two of them - the big cat following - began to trot toward the lake that was becoming visible ahead of them.

"This is the first of the two small lakes I told you about," said Air Walker. "There's really only room in this small canoe for the two of us though and I honestly do NOT want a mountain lion that close to me, right in my canoe, so what about him?"

Golden Eye took time to bathe in the lake, as he had bathed in every body of water so far, before climbing into the canoe.

"Go on, boy, you run around the side of this little lake, okay? We'll stay not too far offshore so you can see us. Good boy, good cat, go that way," he said and pointed up the western shore of the lake.

The big cat looked in the direction Golden Eye pointed then watched as the boy and girl launched the small canoe and began paddling northward. The cougar took a step or two into the water, then, shaking off his paws, retreated onto the shore and began running along the western shore, keeping them in sight.

"Well, I never saw such a thing in my life!" exclaimed Air Walker. "Do you always make pets out of wild animals?"

"Not intentionally," replied Golden Eye. "The old wolf that used to live in this skin just seemed to adopt me when I was little and ran near me wherever I went. He saved my life on my spirit quest too. Then there was a young killer whale that swam up to my canoe one day and took me swimming with him. He helped me rescue my brother from a forest fire and he stopped my....my uncle from killing me one time too. Oh, and there's a black bear that I saved from a pit when he was just a cub. He and I have been friends since then, at least during the summers when he's out of hibernation."

"You what? They what?"

Air Walker stopped paddling in amazement, then put her paddle back into the water, doing her share.

"I know. It's a bit unusual," said Golden Eye.

"A bit unusual! I have never known anyone who had animal friends before! How did this happen?"

"My family tells me I was born with spirit powers, inherited from my ancestors, many of whom were shamans or healers. It's nothing I did myself. I'm just very lucky, I guess."

"Well, lucky is one word for it. Unbelievable is another. I've known people with spirit power too. They go into trances and seem to be told what to do to help our people in times of trouble or sickness, so I do understand spirit power. You must have really inherited a whole lot of it though. I hear that you can even change your shape - transform yourself - like the legends from the time of our ancestors."

"Well, yes. Sometimes when I'm in really big trouble, I connect my spirit with that of my grandfather and I can change into something to help me escape. Luckily I change right back to myself though. I wouldn't want to stay in the shape of a seal or a bird. I like being a boy."

"Okay, here's the end of this little lake. Let's secure this canoe under this brush and look - over there ahead of us to the left. You can just see the sun glinting on the other little lake we have to travel up. Where's your new friend? Ahhh!" yelled Air Walker.

She had turned around from setting the canoe down and there, right beside her, sat Killer Cat, looking her in the eye, albeit a little cross-eyed.

"Great Spirit, keep my heart beating," Air Walker moaned. "I just about died of fright there. I'm never going to get used to that THING creeping up on me like that!"

Then Killer Cat stretched out his neck and rubbed his face on Air Walker's leg.

"Oh my, he's so soft!" she whispered. "I think he likes me too! All right, boy. I trust you," she said and reached out to stroke the cat's head and neck. Still, she gave a little shudder as they stretched their legs and began to trot toward the other lake.

Another canoe was launched and the paddlers set themselves a course for the north end of the lake. Killer Cat bounded off around the west side of it, keeping them in sight most of the time. At some places huge outcroppings of rock jutted out, right into the water. At others the trees were so dense that he just couldn't travel right beside the lake. However, it wasn't long before he was seen again, standing with his forepaws on a log or rock on the shore, watching for Golden Eye's passage.

A short while later, the two paddlers heard a soul-shattering scream! They looked toward where the horrible sound came from and there, atop a high rock bluff, they saw Killer Cat engaged in battle with another cougar. The fight was furious and loud as the two male cats leapt at one another, clawing and tearing, biting and tumbling, high above the lake. Then, in one swift twist, Killer Cat escaped the other cat's grasp, but he slid in the rocky scree and was launched over the edge of the cliff. Down and down he fell, twisting and turning in the air, until he landed with a big splash in the lake.

"Which one of them fell?" called Air Walker.

Golden Eye looked up at the cat on the bluff. The other male mountain lion looked down on his vanquished foe, gave a final hiss, then turned and slunk away, out of sight.

"It was our friend that fell. Let's go and try to help him!" Golden Eye yelled back

The two young people paddled as fast as they could toward Killer Cat. The big cougar surfaced not far from them, puffing and blowing to get a breath of air, while paddling furiously with his paws. His head twisted and turned, seeking the nearest solid land he could set his feet upon.

"This way, boy!" Golden Eye yelled as he paddled toward a flat rock shelf near the north end of the small lake. "Here, you can get out here!," he called, watching over his left shoulder to see if Killer Cat followed. He did.

Golden Eye jumped out onshore as Killer Cat hauled himself out onto the rocky ledge. Golden Eye let his eyes scan the big cat for injury. One of its ears had a tear half a finger long and a patch of fur was missing from the side of his neck, but thankfully Killer Cat's dense fur had prevented the bite from severing the skin and veins of his neck.

"Saghalie Tyee be thanked," Golden Eye whispered. "You're all right boy, aren't you?" he said and he wrapped his arms around his wet, furry friend.

"Golden Eye, lead him over here," called out Air Walker.

She had moved to the head of the canoe and was paddling to a large cleared area near the head of the lake. Golden Eye found a way through the underbrush to Air Walker's landing place. He watched behind himself to be sure that Killer Cat followed. The big cat was limping a little on his right foreleg but he trusted Golden Eye and followed him, although his big head twisted quickly around at every rustle of bushes near him.

The sun was nearly set when they dragged their canoe up onto the northern shore of the second small lake so they quickly set about making a windbreak shelter and sleeping pads of cedar boughs for the oncoming night. Air Walker got a fire going with dry, dead wood, leaves and small twigs and her flint rocks. Then she added larger bits of branches that Golden Eye gathered up.

Killer Cat, after shaking and licking himself dry a little, surprised them by going off into the forest and returning with a fat rabbit which he dropped at Golden Eye's feet. His own mouth was rimed with blood so it was obvious he had eaten his own kill first, then brought another for his adopted family.

"Many thanks, boy!" exclaimed Golden Eye, as he ruffled the fur around Killer Cat's ears. "You're a big helper, aren't you? I'm surprised you'd go hunting with that other big cat nearby. Pretty brave, aren't you?"

Killer Cat turned his head, leaning into the rub. Then he lay down at the edge of the firelight and began to wash himself - his lips and jowls, licking his paws and rubbing them over his head, then the fur of his chest, his paws and his sides, then as much of his back as he could reach. When his self-bath was done, he gave a big sigh and laid right down and closed his eyes.

"Washed off the last traces of your battle, have you, my friend?" asked the boy.

Golden Eye got busy skinning the rabbit then skewered it on a green stick. After that he jammed the stick into the ground beside the fire, securing it with some rocks, so that the meat was over the fire. He and Air Walker took turns going off to bathe and watching or turning the roasting meat.

"Here," said Air Walker. "Here's your half of the rabbit," she said as she passed the delicious smelling meat to Golden Eye on a clean cedar frond. "Sorry about the rough serving dish."

"That's all right. I like 'wilderness dishes' just fine, thank you," replied Golden Eye. And my hand makes a fine cup for water, as does yours. Here's some huckleberries for you. I found a bush with a few left. I guess the local bears forgot a few. They sure love those things, don't they?"

"Yes, they sure do. We don't go far into the woods when they're all fattening up on berries before their long winter sleep. You never want to get between a momma bear and her cubs. Even if you don't mean them any harm, those sow bears get a really nasty attitude when they have cubs to protect, right?" said Air Walker, stifling a yawn.

"Oh, I know that from recent experience," Golden Eye chuckled.

He'd been struggling to keep his eyes open too. So, they banked up the fire with some thick branches and chunks of fallen trees, curled up under their respective coverings and listened to the mad, laughter-like call of loons out upon the mist-shrouded lake.

"Tell me about your friend that you're meeting at my village," said Air Walker sleepily.

"Tan Buck?" replied Golden Eye. "Oh, he's the best. The best friend I've ever had. The best friend anyone could ever have. He's stronger than I am and he's funny too. He gets so excited sometimes that he forgets to be careful and ends up in a mess. Oh, the great times we've had together! Before my vision quest we used to race all over the Island of Salty Springs. We'd climb up Crouching Mountain and sing our secret chant and see the whole world, we thought. One time though, we went down the back way and ended up in a haunted cave. I saved his life on the way down to it when the rocks gave way.

Oh, and another time we nearly got sucked into a really big whirlpool, and he was with me when I found my killer whale friend. Then there was the time his soul got lost and I helped get it back. And our adventures here on Protector Island too, with our cousin Big Head, when Killer Cat started chasing us, and the Thunderbird defeating the giant, supernatural Killer Whale too. Oh yes, we've been through a lot together and I'm really looking forward to seeing him soon at your village."

"'I can't wait to meet him," yawned Air Walker. "It really does sound like you two are great friends."

Golden Eye drifted off to sleep to the gentle sounds of the lake lapping onshore, the fire crackling, the soft snores of the cat and the girl. He couldn't help smiling as he gave way to slumber.

Chapter Twenty

Storm on the Lake

Golden Eye awoke to a strange sensation - like harsh dogfish skin scraping his face! He opened his eyes and raised his hand to his face. His hand met fur and his eyes were staring right into those of Killer Cat - not one hand width from his! Killer Cat's warm breath bathed Golden Eye's face.

Golden Eye sat up and wrapped his arms around the neck of the beautiful beast.

"Good morning, boy," he said cheerily.

Killer Cat rubbed his face along the side of Golden Eye's head.

"Time to get up and get going, is it, big fellow?" Golden Eye asked.

Air Walker woke up, sighed, rolled over and watched boy and cat. She sat up and shook her head.

"I still can't believe that a great big mountain lion like that could just switch from hunting you down for days and days, intent on killing you - maybe even eating you - to loving you like he does now. It's absolutely astounding!" she muttered sleepily. "Oooh, my shoulders and arms are all stiff and sore, are yours?"

"Yes, mine are a little sore too, but not bad. I've probably been doing more paddling than you lately, though." he replied. "Well, let's get up and get going. How far to that big lake? Can we cross it in one day, do you think?"

"Well, we have to paddle down that river to get to Nimpkish Lake, that'll take quite a while as it wanders around the mountains and hills. Then the lake itself. It's much larger than the two little ones we crossed yesterday. So, I think we'd be very lucky to make it all the way across it by tonight - maybe halfway, I'd guess," said Air Walker, all the while rolling up her blanket.

"All right then. Let's get washed and eat a few berries, have a drink from that cool spring and then get on our way. What do you think, my furry friend?" he said while stroking Killer Cat's soft, tawny back.

Killer Cat just sat down and waited expectantly to see what the young people were going to do. He didn't have to wait long. They bathed, ate and broke camp in short order and were about to set off down the river on the last leg of their journey.

Before they launched their canoe, however,

Killer Cat did a strange thing. He walked up to Golden Eye, bumped his head against the boy's hip, licked his hand then turned and began to track off southward.

"What's he doing?" asked Air Walker in surprise.

"I think he's going home," said Golden Eye and an immense sadness came over him. "I guess that fight with the other mountain lion made him realize that he's way out of his own territory so he's heading for his own place."

"Oh, my. Well, I'm surprised to hear myself say this, but I'm going to miss him too, really, I am!" said the girl.

Golden Eye ran after Killer Cat and got down on his knees in front of him. He buried his face in the cougar's warm coat, winning himself a last friendly purr and lick of his face, then he stood and watched his enemy-become-friend go on his way. When he could no longer see the tawny fur, the proud head and the black tip of Killer Cat's tail, Golden Eye turned and went back to where Air Walker waited by the canoe. She silently placed a hand on his shoulder, showing him that she understood his loss.

The sky changed from sunny to overcast as they paddled along but still it was a good day to travel so far. The river narrowed into near rapids or spread out lazily, depending on the surrounding landscape. By mid-day, they entered the big lake. They stopped for a

short break, bathing, eating and drinking to refresh themselves. Then they pushed off into the heart of the lake.

A flock of mallards took off as they passed them, flapping their wings rapidly. The beautiful green heads of the males glowed in the pale sunlight.

"This really is a big lake, isn't it?" asked Golden Eye.

"Yes," Air Walker smilingly answered. "But you should be able to make it if I can," she teased.

"Well then, let's see you take lead paddle if you think you're so good," he called back over his shoulder.

"Certainly," she replied. "Let's switch now."

Very carefully, they changed places and Air Walker set a brisk paddling pace so that Golden Eye really did have to work to keep up with her.

On and on they paddled, as the afternoon wore away. They kept up their challenge of each other, throwing taunts back and forth from time to time.

Late in the day, though, as they mutually agreed to take a few moments to rest their arms, they took a good look around. What they saw was not at all reassuring. They were a long way from any shore and the lake around them was being churned up into green, angry-looking wavelets. The sun could no longer be seen behind a grey, lowering bank of clouds. The wind was rushing at them in harsh gusts and they were pelted with rain. The canoe began to bob about in a worrisome manner.

"Which way to shore?" Golden Eye yelled.

"We'd better head into the wind so we don't get swamped," Air Walker called back. "And you'd better take lead paddle, I'm getting tired."

"All right," he replied and they very gingerly switched places.

Golden Eye really put his back into the paddling now, heading into the wind enough to keep the canoe upright yet still make some headway up the lake.

On they paddled as the sky darkened even more. They began to be pelted with sleet too, a nasty mix of snow and freezing rain. The two took turns taking a moment to don their capes and waterproof hats that the Nuu-chah-nulth women had woven for them and strap their belongings tight to their bodies.

"That's better," called Golden Eye to his companion. "Can you see the shore yet?"

"I think we're not too far now," she yelled back over the howl of the storm. "These waves are getting awfully big. I hope we make it."

The words were hardly out of her mouth when a sharp blast of wind from hit them, followed by a rogue wave that washed over top of Air Walker and filled the canoe. Air Walker instinctively rose to get her head above water and the canoe overturned, tossing them both into the frigid, green, wave-tossed water.

"Air Walker!" Golden Eye called out. "Where are you?"

"Here!" she screamed from the back edge of the

canoe. "Help me, I don't want to die!"

Golden Eye, in trouble himself, trying to keep his head up above the tossing waves, felt his spirit connect with that of his grandfather, the shaman.

"What shall I do, old wise one?" his spirit asked.

"In the lake are good spirits. Call to them," came his answer.

Golden Eye gathered all his spirit power together as he made his way back along the edge of the canoe to hold on to Air Walker and his soul called out for aid.

Then, out of the blackness of the storm, up from the depths of the lake arose a great shining mat that lifted the boy and the girl and bore them up.

"What is this?" Air Walker screamed.

"It's the trout! It's all the trout in this lake, come to save us," Golden Eye yelled back.

Air Walker went on screaming. She didn't know whether she was more afraid of the lake and the storm or of this shining, heaving, wriggling silver mass beneath her. She didn't stop screaming until she felt herself flung forward as she and Golden Eye landed in a heap upon the westward shore of the lake.

As the storm raged on, the two bedraggled young people coughed and spit and wrung out their things. But, before they moved on, before they made a fire or burrowed into a big sheltering hollow fallen tree, before they made themselves hot tea, Golden Eye and Air Walker stopped. They stood on the shore of the

lake and gave thanks from the depths of their souls to
the Great Spirit, Saghalie Tyee, to the spirit of the lake
trout and to Grandfather Strong Oak for their safety.

Golden Eye held Air Walker's arm as she
walked unsteadily back to their makeshift shelter.

"I-I've never been s-s-o c-c-close to d-death
before," came from her shivering blue lips.

"Well, at least you didn't just float away,"
Golden Eye jested, trying to make her smile. "How
would I have managed, trying to hold you down and

paddle too?"

Air Walker chuckled shakily as she huddled over the fire, shivering and rubbing her arms and legs to get them warm.

"What about the canoe?" she asked.

"Don't worry about that," calmly replied Golden Eye, drying himself by the fire too. "In the morning, if the storm is over, I'll swim out and turn it back upright and bring it in. You know it will float even upside down or full of water."

"All right, that's g-g-good," said Air Walker, reassured by his calm tone.

Golden Eye kept his own feelings to himself. He was concerned about how long the storm would last, about how far away the canoe might have drifted, and also about Killer Cat. Was he safe on his homeward journey? And would Tan Buck be ready for their own voyage home from the village of the Kwakwaka'wakw? He had trouble getting dry and warm enough to fall asleep that night.

Chapter Twenty-One

Journey's End

Honk! Honk, honk, ho-honk, ho-honk!

Golden Eye awoke to the sound of a big vee of Canada geese skimming the treetops above their burrow. The storm was over. Air Walker too stretched and yawned and dragged herself into consciousness.

"Well, they're in a hurry aren't they?" she observed.

"I guess that first blast of winter reminded them to head for a warmer place, and the sooner the better! We should follow their example and get going to your village, don't you think?" Golden Eye asked.

"Absolutely. This is turning out to be not so much fun."

"You can say that again."

"This is turning out...."

"All right, all right, funny girl. Let's look around and see what damage there was from the storm."

They banked up the fire, ate a little dried meat from their packs, hung up their blankets to dry and then walked down to the shore of Nimpkish Lake.

In the bright morning sunlight they shaded their eyes and scanned the surface of the lake for the canoe. Golden Eye climbed up on a huge granite boulder to get a better view.

"I don't believe it!" he exclaimed. "Look, over there to the left. The canoe has washed up into the river inlet all by itself!"

"We are really lucky," enthused Air Walker. "This lake drains into that small river and it runs right out to my village. Let's bail that thing out and get on our way. Suddenly I can't wait to see my family, even my annoying little brothers."

Golden Eye laughed at that, remembering his own little busybody of a brother, Fat Goose, and his baby sister, Silent Dawn. He laughed, then he felt a surge of homesickness himself. With a sigh, he shrugged it off and got busy. He and Air Walker righted the canoe and bailed it out. Fortunately the bailers and paddles had washed up on shore too, although it took some time to find them amidst the overhanging brush at the lakeside. The activity and the warm sun helped though, warming them, easing their stiff muscles and pushing away the nightmare of yesterday's storm. Food, warmth, and companionship all combined to make life good again.

Within a handsbreadth of the sun's journey across the sky, Golden Eye and Air Walker were on their way, on the last leg of their journey together. The river ran full and fast due to the night of rain and they sped along, carefully dodging rocky outcroppings and churning back eddys. Golden Eye couldn't resist raising his paddle and giving a big whoop of excitement from time to time, remembering similar adventures with Tan Buck.

"It won't be long now," yelled Air Walker. "My home is just around that bend up there."

Golden Eye looked over his shoulder at Air Walker's face and, just as he suspected, it was glowing with joy. He dug in with his paddle, determined to get her home as quickly as he could.

And then, there it was! Xwalk, the grand village of the Kwakwaka'wakw. Golden Eye was astonished and enchanted with the sight of it. Set among giant cedar trees that dripped with moss, stretching far along the coast of Protector Island and onto the offshore islands were many, many longhouses. Four here, five there, on and on, the village spread, facing this inner stretch of the Western Ocean.

The wind gently sighing through the trees, the salty ocean breeze, the croaking caws of ravens, rising smoke and the sound of people - many, many people - filled Golden Eye's senses. Such a shock it was, to be in the midst of humanity again after what seemed like a long time in the lonely wilderness, with no one to rely on but themselves, other than the odd meal provided by Killer Cat.

"I hope you're safely home, boy," Golden Eye whispered, thinking of the big cat.

Air Walker scarcely helped beach the canoe when she ran at full speed toward what must be her own home, her parents' longhouse.

"I'll just say hello to my mother and I'll be right back out, wait here!" she yelled.

Golden Eye slowly approached. He stared open-mouthed at the enormity of the Kwakwaka'wakw village. These longhouses were different from those of his home and of the Nuu-chah-nulth. The boards of the sides stood upright. As he drew nearer he saw that the tops and bottoms of these planks were tapered to fit into slots in the roof beams and the bottom boards. Some of the roof beams had their ends carved in family crests such as the sea lion. Certain of the rear houseposts were elaborately carved in the Kwakwaka'wakw style depicting Thunderbird and other family protector spirits.

As he moved around to the front of the seemingly endless line of longhouses he noticed that some, probably those of the clan chiefs, had their entire front decorated in black and red with clan designs. There were also intricately carved totem poles at the centre front of the longhouses, some poles even having great, gaping archways serving as the entrances to the homes. People were moving about busily - very busily. "Must be preparing for yet another potlatch," Golden Eye smiled, remembering what Air Walker had told him about the almost constant state of one potlatch after another in her village. Suddenly he heard a loud yell.

"Golden Eye! Is that you? Is that really you?"

A group of big boys and young men were coming back from the foreshore and one separated from the bunch and came running full tilt toward Golden Eye. It was Tan Buck! Golden Eye felt a great rush of happiness at seeing him, his best friend since their earliest childhood. He charged toward Tan Buck and wrapped his friend in a big hug. As the rest of the group came toward them, the two friends laughed and yelled and thumped each other on the back.

"How are you?"

"What took you so long to get here?"

"Look at you, you're taller already than when I last saw you!"

"How was the trip?"

"What have you been doing here?"

Their words tumbled over one another in their excitement to empty their heads of all the questions that sprang to their lips after such a long time away from each other. Indeed, they had both grown a little taller; their hair had grown some and each had an air about them of having had more life experiences; ones they hadn't shared for once.

"Golden Eye, all of us boys were just playing a great game, come and play it with us." exclaimed Tan Buck.

Tan Buck quickly introduced Golden Eye to all his new friends, including Swims-With-Seals who had accompanied him to the village. Golden Eye greeted all the boys and young men, somewhat amazed at the size of the group. However, glancing back at the great long village, it became obvious that a village of many hundreds of people would certainly have this many young people and more!

A dozen of the boys agreed to go back to the beach for the game and the rest excused themselves, citing chores waiting for them, what with another pot-latch coming up. Tan Buck, Golden Eye and the other willing players raced back down to the shore.

"All right, first, we have to collect some kelp. There's a bed of it just offshore," instructed Tan Buck. "Good. Get lots. We just want the bulbs and the tube part, leave the leaves. Now, half of us make stacks of sections of tubes here and the other half make your stack over there, about thirty paces apart. Next, take all the bulbs and hide them behind the stacks of tubes. All right. Now, we take turns, one from each team at a time, throwing these spears we made and try to spear a tube or better yet, a bulb. If you spear a tube, you get to bring it back and put it on our pile, protecting our bulb 'heads'.

The winning team is the one that 'captures' ten bulb heads first. Understand? All right, let's go, and make sure to stay well out of the way of thrown spears. Some of these guys are really bad shots," teased Tan Buck.

Several of the other boys promptly swarmed all over Tan Buck, sitting him down and tickling him mercilessly for a minute as punishment for the teasing.

Golden Eye watched the fun with a smile then helped his old friend to his feet. After that they all settled down to the serious business of the game.

"This would be great practice for learning to harpoon like the Nuu-chah-nulth did," Golden Eye observed to Tan Buck.

"I'll bet you have lots of tales to tell about that, haven't you?" queried Tan Buck.

"I sure do!" exclaimed Golden Eye.

The boys rushed back and forth across the beach gathering up kelp and making stacks of tubes and piles of bulbs. They found and checked their spears and made one for Golden Eye and the fun was on. There was plenty of shouting and laughter as the boys pierced each others' tubes and captured each others' bulbs. Tan Buck's throws were arrow straight and he became the champion.

When the game was over, the boys led Golden

Eye back to the village where Air Walker was waiting to introduce Golden Eye to her family and share a meal with her traveling companion. Golden Eye saw that she had already bathed and put on a new apron and a robe of woven goat hair and cedar.

"Tonight, at the big gathering after the evening meal, you and I can tell everyone of our adventures," whispered Air Walker. "Right now, bring your friend with you and let's get some real food into us. I'm starving."

"I am too," said Golden Eye and they tucked into a good, hot dish of steamed halibut, camas roots and wild onions. Tan Buck, always hungry, ate his share too.

Round the campfire that night, the Kwakwaka'wakw people marvelled at their many tales of adventure; but even after hours of sharing stories around the fire and meeting so many of the fine people of the massive Xwalk village, Golden Eye and Tan Buck still had many things to say and to share with each other.

Tan Buck had to see the scars on Golden Eye's shoulder and arm. He wanted minute details of the encounters with Killer Cat and the whaling expedition, Snake Woman and the Wolf Society ceremony. On into the night they talked. They had chosen to sleep in the forest under a tree, feet facing east like Stutsun, so that they didn't disturb others trying to sleep.

"What was it like here, over the past moon?" Golden Eye asked his friend, his head propped up on one forearm.

"It's been great! There was a potlatch just after I got here. Swims-With-Seals' father is head chief of the Kawas tribe. That name means Murderers! Can you believe it? A long time ago, two chiefs quarreled over a bet and the argument never got settled. Things escalated until one tried to kill the other. He failed and then was lured into death by the other chief. The one that won became known as the Murderer and people took sides about it and ever since the winning chief's family tribe has been known as the Kawas - the Murderers. You'd never know it now though; they all get along perfectly well. Oh, except for the potlatch competitions. You have never seen anything like it. They have to have whole buildings to store up the blankets, canoes, carvings, oil, food and shells that they give away!"

"How do they ever get so much together?" asked the incredulous Golden Eye.

"Well, say you get twenty blankets as a gift. You loan them out to someone who's hosting a potlatch. Then you have to be paid back double when you are collecting up stuff for your own potlatch a year or two later. In the meantime you and your family are creating lots of things yourselves. You never saw such a group for decorating! You saw all the wonderful totem poles, didn't you? Every one of them tells of that family or that chief's heroic feats or encounters with supernatural beings and their family crests. Oh, and they have special totems for burials too. White ones."

To the soft hoots of owls and the sound of scurrying night creatures, the two best friends drifted off to sleep. For both of them their last thought was of how good it was to be together again, two young Salish in the land of the Kwakwaka'wakw.

Shafts of sunlight pierced the cedar fronds and woke the sleeping friends and they grinned at each other. The sight of a long-known, familiar face was so precious, so special. All the days and years, all the adventures they had shared together and now their separate experiences rekindled the bond between them.

"Come on, lets go for a swim while the tide's in," said Tan Buck.

"I'm right behind you," enthused Golden Eye.

The two friends whooped and yelled as their sleep warmed bodies hit the cold, green ocean. Small waves were rolling in as the boys and some of their new friends swam out, turned and surfed back to shore on the crests of the waves. To his surpirse and delight, Golden Eye noticed a dolphin on each side of him, riding the surf too. The other boys watched incredulously as the dolphins rubbed against Golden Eye's sides and towed him back to deeper water as he held onto their dorsal fins. After a while, they flipped up out of the water, nodded and chuckled at Golden Eye and departed.

A crowd had formed to watch the spectacle and it wasn't long before they were joined by what seemed like two hundred people. Golden Eye's mind was boggled by the sight of so many villagers.

He and Tan Buck rinsed off the salt in a tumbling, splashing stream - quickly, because competition for rinsing time was fierce. Then off they went to see who had some breakfast ready. Air Walker waved to them from her family's longhouse and they needed no further invitation.

"A beautiful day the Great Spirit has given us, isn't it?" she greeted them. "Come and see what mother and I have prepared for the morning meal."

"Now don't think I make all this every day," explained Woman-from-the-North, Air Walker's mother. "We're having a special welcome feast for you and Air Walker tonight."

She proceeded to place several small bowls before the three young people. There were three kinds of white fish in one bowl that Golden Eye recognized as red snapper, rock cod and halibut, fresh and succulent. Another bowl held smoked salmon, clams and oysters with a tiny bowl of oolachon oil in which to dip them. They were served water before they ate and after they ate but did not drink while eating, in the way of the Kwakwaka'wakw.

"What's for after food?" asked Air Walker.

"After food?" said the two boys together.

"Yes, we always have something special, just to finish the meal and freshen up the mouth after eating fish. Oooh look, dried blackberry and blueberry cakes! Thank you mother."

"Yes, thank you very much," said Golden Eye. I've never had such a wonderful morning meal."

"Yes," agreed Tan Buck. If tonight's food is anything like this, I'd say we're in for a real feast, don't you think, Golden Eye?"

"Absolutely! Can we do anything for you to repay you for this wonderful meal?"

"No need to repay. Hungry children have to be fed and guests always get the best there is," said Woman-from-the-North shyly. "But, if you want to be some help to me, you can go and get me some more firewood and fill up these seal bladders with fresh water. I'd appreciate that."

"We'd be happy to. Let's go, old friend," said Golden Eye.

"Here, I'll stack wood on your arms," offered Tan Buck.

"Who's going to stack wood on your arms?"

"Hey, I'm going to be carrying water! It's heavier than wood."

"Is not."

"Is too."

The friends carried on, carrying wood and water, bantering and bumping one another; each trying to make the other drop his load until they delivered them to Woman-of-the-North.

Then off they went in a whirl of introductions. Every family greeted Golden Eye warmly, many of them exclaiming over his swim with the dolphins. Tan Buck hastened to brag that his friend also swam with a killer whale, ran with wolves and had a bear friend as well.

"That's enough, Tan Buck," Golden Eye would protest. "I'm sorry that you couldn't have met my latest friend, the Killer Cat. A good bonk on the head changed him from killer to cuddly, just like that!" Golden Eye explained to Tan Buck and their new friends.

"Maybe you'll meet him again, on your way home," suggested Man-of-Many-Potlatches, the chief of the Thunderbird clan.

The tide had run out and back in during the course of the day. Then, as it began to run out again, as little waves rolled calmly up onto the shore and disappeared, Golden Eye watched the sunset-coloured clouds race by. Behind him stood the forest of giant cedars and a forest of longhouses; before him lay the ocean shore, laced with gnarly driftwood, many-coloured sea shells and skittering shorebirds seeking the harvest of the tidal flats.

Off toward the Great Land he gazed at islands big and small, drenched in the last golden rays of the sun. Paddlers were coming in long canoes from the big island not far offshore where stood a good-sized village; smoke still rising from their fires.

Far into the evening, the feasting and story-telling went on but the two friends finally wandered off to their sleeping mats. They said goodnight and drifted off into slumber, dreaming of adventures and wonderful, wonderful food.

Chapter Twenty-Two

Captured!

The next morning Golden Eye awoke late. His mind was still full of the events of the past evening as he opened his eyes. Yes, there he was, safe and sound in a corner of Air Walker's family's longhouse. Some of the family were still asleep too. Some had arisen and were building up the fires. They had blankets wrapped around their shoulders to ward off the chill of the coming winter.

Golden Eye stretched and rolled over to wake up Tan Buck. He was greatly surprised to see that Tan Buck's bed was empty. His friend usually loved his sleep and needed to be prodded into wakefulness. Golden Eye sat up and looked around.

"If you're looking for your friend, he's gone fishing with Swims-With-Seals and another boy. They didn't want to wake you up because you were sleeping so soundly. Would you like some breakfast?" Woman-of-the-North asked kindly.

"Thank you. I'll just go and wash up first and be right back. Shall I bring back some more water?"

"That would be good. Here's a seal bladder."

Golden Eye went off to the fresh water stream and washed himself, filled the bladder and returned to eat a little steamed salmon, followed by a huckleberry cake and a big draught of fresh, clear water. He thanked Air Walker's mother then went off in search of his friend.

Golden Eye asked various people who were near the shore if they knew which way Swims-With-Seals had headed to fish. Some hadn't seen the boys. One thought they had headed southward but one man said that he had definitely seen them headed northward, pointing toward a cluster of rocks that rose just above the surface. There was good cod fishing there, he said.

Golden Eye wandered along the shore, heading northward, into a strong breeze, to see if he could see the boys in their canoe. As he passed one longhouse after another he was hailed and greeted by one new acquaintance after another. From time to time he paused to talk with someone.

He wandered on 'til he was beyond the last longhouse. He scanned the water, able to see three sides of the rocky outcrop as he traveled. He saw no sign of the boys. The wind was beginning to blow quite strongly.

Then he stumbled on a boulder and, as his eyes turned to look for proper footing, he saw a paddle. One paddle, then another he saw. One was of the pointed Kwakwaka'wakw style and the other one of his own maple paddles, carved by his Uncle Raven Claw!

Golden Eye picked up the paddles. Worry and fear were beginning to form in his mind. He let his eyes scan the shoreline, hoping to find the boys, hoping they were all right. He laid down the paddles above the tide line and began running along the shore, calling out his friends' names. On and on he ran, far up the shore then back along the edge of the forest, then down the shore toward the village.

People of the village began to hear his shouts and came out of their longhouses and away from their various pursuits.

"What's wrong?" came a chorus of voices.

"Something. Something's wrong. I couldn't see the boys or their canoe but I found their paddles on the shore, away up there. Has anyone seen them?"

"No, not lately."

"No, I haven't, have you?" he heard people say.

"Let's get some canoes and go look for them," said one of the men.

Quick as a flash, canoes were launched and they fanned out in all directions. The wind was making the water very choppy now and they had to be careful not to get swamped. Golden Eye was in a ten-man canoe that headed northward. They circled the rocky outcrop for which the missing boys had been heading.

"Look. Up on the rocks there!" yelled Golden Eye.

The men steered the canoe up to the rocks, carefully balancing with their paddles as Golden Eye jumped ashore. "Isn't this Swims-With-Seals' cape?" he asked. "It has blood and a hole here, see?"

The men all looked at the cape and passed it to each other, while still struggling to keep their canoe steady in the rapidly rising waves.

"Yes, that's his cape, for sure," said one young man whom Golden Eye recognized as Swims-With-Seals' brother. "I'm afraid they've been taken by raiders from the north."

"Well, let's go and get them back!" cried Golden Eye.

"I'm sorry but we can't go after them right now," said one of the older men. "There's a really big storm building up for one thing. We'll be lucky to get back to the village actually."

"When we do, we'll have to talk with all the men and decide what to do about this and when," said another man.

"What do you mean, what and when?" cried the distraught Golden Eye. "We have to go and get them right away!"

"Like I said, it's not possible now. We'd all like-

ly die in this storm. Let's get back home while we still can."

Golden Eye's mind and heart were reeling in agony. He paddled with the rest of the men but kept looking back over his shoulder, northward, into the gale, where his friend was gone.

Back at the great Xwalk village of the Kwakwaka'wakw, a council of all the elders was called. Golden Eye listened as they discussed the whole situation. After what seemed to him a long time, the council was ended and he was drawn aside by the Great Chief of the Whale clan.

"My boy, you must understand the whole situation here. The bad storms of winter are upon us now. Two of the search canoes were swamped today, just looking around here for those boys. The winter storms are much worse for us up here than for your village way down south, protected as it is.

Also, in order to get your friend and our boys back, we'd have to go as a war party and fight with the people from the north, the Haida. Even as many as we are, and as brave as we are, the Haida are formidable foes. We will have to prepare all winter and make a plan for rescuing those boys.

Don't be too worried. They have probably been taken as slaves, not killed. They are good strong boys and if they behave themselves, they should be safe."

Golden Eye looked into the eyes of the old chief

and knew that what he was saying was true but his heart grieved. He remembered his grandmother's story; that she and her brother had been taken as slaves and that she had escaped and had to run a long, long way until his grandfather found her. Golden Eye knew that her life as a slave had been very hard so he couldn't bear the thought of Tan Buck being a slave.

"Well, I understand all that you have said," he said sadly to the chief. "I understand, but I have to do something! I will take my small canoe as soon as this storm is over and go to the very north end of Protector Island. From there, when I can see that there is going to be good weather for a whole day, I am going to paddle out toward the islands of the Haida. If I am lucky, I will go ashore secretly and try to find the boys. If they catch me and take me as a slave too, then I will be with Tan Buck and the others and maybe together we can find a way to escape. I'm sorry, but I can't just stay here. I have to do something!"

"You are being foolish. It is many days travel to the land of the Haida; many miles of open ocean where storms come up quickly. Think of your family. They are expecting you home now. What will they think of your dangerous plan?"

"Please send them a message. Tell them that I won't be home until, or unless, I can bring Tan Buck with me. Ask my grandfather to send me spirit power and to be with me in times of danger. Don't worry too much. I am very strong with the spirit world. They will help me, the spirit of the wolf and the killer whale. Goodbye."

Golden Eye gathered his belongings and his canoe and prepared to set out to make himself a winter camp at the north end of Protector Island. He vowed to be ready to travel to the land of the Haida to rescue his lifelong friend the very first moment he could. He sent his spirit soaring to Tan Buck.

"I'm coming, my friend. I'll come and get you. Don't give up. Don't die. I'll be there soon!"

Glossary

adept . . . . .skilled
adze . . . . .curve-bladed, axe-like tool
compensation . . . . .something given in replacement
deranged . . . . .wild or crazy
envoy . . . . .messenger or representative
forbears . . . . .ancestors, those that went before
hermit . . . . .person living apart from all others
kindred . . . . .family relative
leviathan . . . . .very large or powerful creature
migration . . . . .seasonal moving to another place
nemesis . . . . .enemy, causing one's downfall
nocturnal . . . . .of the night time
obsidian . . . . .hard, glassy, volcanic rock
perished . . . . .died
pervaded . . . . .spread throughout
phenomenon . . . . .a remarkable person or thing
raucous . . . . .loud and harsh
shaman . . . . .healer and religious leader
stalactite . . . . .tapering, downhanging column
stalagmite . . . . . . .tapering, uprising column
stoically . . . . .bravely, showing no pain or fear
talisman . . . . .lucky charm
thong . . . . .narrow strip of leather
traverse . . . . .travel across or through
travois . . . . .carrying device made of poles
woebegone . . . . . .sad or miserable in appearance

Bibliography

Indian Myths and Legends from the North Pacific Coast of America / Franz Boas/Talon Books
Smoke From Their Fires, The Life of a Kwakiutl Chief
Clellan S. Ford/Waveland Press, Inc.
The Whales of Canada
Erich Hoyt/Camden House Publishers Ltd.
Indian Herbalogy of North America
Alma R. Hutchens/Merco
The Wisdom of The Elders: Native Traditions on the Northwest Coast
Ruth Kirk/Douglas & McIntyre Ltd.
Handbook of American Indian Games
Allan Macfarlan/New York, Dover
Since The Time of the Transformers: The Ancient Heritage of the Nuu-chah-nulth, Ditidaht and Makah
Alan D. McMillan/Douglas & McIntyre
Those Who Fell From The Sky
Daniel D. Marshall/Rainshadow Press
The First Nations of B.C.: An Anthropological Survey
Robert J. Muckle/UBC Press
The Gulf Islands Explorer-The Complete Guide
Bruce Obee/Gray's Publishing
Cedar
Hilary Stewart/Douglas & McIntyre
Seafaring Warriors of the West: Nootka Indians
D.F. Symington/Ginn

About The Author

Judith Moody was born in Vancouver, British Columbia, Canada, the third of seven children in a big happy family of which Grandma was always a part. Being very, very shy, Judith ran home from school each day for lunch with Mom and to hear story-time on the radio. Books became her best friends - especially children's adventure books. She was read to by her big sister and so Judith read to her little brothers, sharing the magic of books. School, Sunday School, Brownies and Guides, plus loving, involved parents taught her life's good lessons. Her grandmother had spirit power and a little of that was passed along in the family.

She grew up to become a wife and mother and the family enjoyed camping and boating in British Columbia's beautiful outdoors. People she met, places she saw, and legends she learned led her to want to capture and share the magic with children everywhere. Her own children and grandchildren have some First Nations heritage too, so making her hero a Coast Salish boy seemed very natural. She hopes you will read, enjoy and share Golden Eye's adventures.

Judith studied with and received her diploma from the Institute of Children's Literature and is a member of the Society of Children's Book Writers and Illustrators.

Also by the Author
Golden Eye and the Deadly Dancer

Travelling back to the long-ago days when the spirit world was much closer, we meet Golden Eye on his way to his vision quest. A raging forest fire delays his trip and he must rescue his brother and an injured deer. He is aided by his orca friend and then uses his spirit power to save the village. We reflect back then on when and how he came by his spirit power and its consequences in his life.

Golden Eye is an adventurer; full of eagerness to learn of his land and people and to strengthen his spirit powers. He and his best friend Tan Buck go adventuring all over and around their home on the Island of Salty Springs, off the west coast of Canada. Exploring a haunted gold cave, climbing mountains, white-water canoeing, swimming with an orca are all part of this first book of Golden Eye's adventures. Share the fun and danger as he creates a children's potlatch, communes with the Great Spirit, plays ancient games, shares legends, and makes up his own stories. Sharing with his family and village relatives, learning from his shaman grandfather and medicine woman grandmother, helping build his own canoe, rescuing his friend's soul from the spirit world and finally going on his vision quest are all part of the grand adventures of this brave young lad.